DARE DARKER

A BLACK ROSE COLLECTION NOVEL

PEPPER NORTH

PUBLISHING

When the daylight fades and time stands still.
The feeling of flying from just one touch.
Moving slowly, kissing softly.
The flash of fever, becoming lost in the flames.
Surrendering.
Going under.
These are the moments that leave us breathless.

Introducing a brand-new collection of romance books by
independently published and USA Today bestselling authors whose
words will leave you breathless! The *Leave Me Breathless* books
promise to bring you stories of love, passion, betrayal, and hope...and
always a happily ever after!
Plus, each collection is themed so you can easily shop for what you're
in the mood to read! Want a sports romance? Check out the Ivy
Collection! Or how about a dark romantic suspense? The Black Rose
Collection has you covered!

THE COLLECTIONS:

The Moonflower Collection
The Moonflower symbolizes dreaming of love. These books feature
enemies-to-lovers romance, insta-love, virgin romance, and romantic
comedy.

The Ivy Collection

The Ivy symbolizes dependence, endurance, and faithfulness. These books feature sports romances, rockstar romances, military, and single parent.

The Black Rose Collection

The darker side of Leave Me Breathless...

The Black Rose symbolizes rejuvenation or rebirth, but it can also symbolize death and farewell. These books feature dark romantic suspense, BDSM themes, true crime, dark military, dark MC, and Mafia.

The Lilac Collection

The Lilac symbolizes the first emotion in love. These books feature new adult romance, second chance romance, and prequels to an existing series.

For more books and authors in the Leave Me Breathless Collection, please visit WWW.LEAVEMEBREATHLESSBOOKS.COM.

DARE DARKER

A Black Rose Collection Novel

by Pepper North

1

Rafael cued up the video one more time. There was something that drew him to the brunette who crossed the lobby with his sales manager. A hint of vulnerability masked under cheerful bravado drew his attention. The way she looked into the darkened corners of the room challenged him to notice her and act. Picking up the phone, he selected a number.

"Offer apartment 961 to Mia Daniels. She toured a smaller apartment on the second floor on Monday," Rafael Montalvo instructed his manager. "Set the price at the same cost."

"But Mr. Montalvo, that apartment is much larger, and the view is spectacular. If you are ready to rent that apartment, we can get a much higher fee," the manager rushed to correct him.

"I'm afraid you didn't understand my wishes. Contact Ms. Daniels and offer her the apartment for the same rent as the one she toured." Rafael was not one to have his wishes questioned—ever. He did not appreciate being second-guessed. As the other man stammered an assurance that he would make the call today, Rafael texted his administrative assistant. The message was simple: *Select a new manager for my apartment building to begin within the month.*

Disconnecting as the man blathered on, still wasting his time,

Rafael replayed the video again. After consulting the private investigator's report, he'd made up his mind. She was the one he had been seeking. It was just as his father had described recognizing his future bride. Mia would be his.

His second phone call was the cleaning service he regularly employed when staying in the city. They would prepare the penthouse apartment in the beautiful building for his imminent arrival. While he could observe her movements from anywhere in the world, Rafael needed to be close to her.

Already, he believed that she was his. Now, she would need to prove her suitability—to earn her place in his life. They would meet soon.

The willowy brunette let herself into her beautiful apartment. She'd lived there for almost six months. It hadn't been the first place she'd seen in the complex. Mia Daniels had actually toured a much smaller studio apartment in the fancy building. To her delight, the facility manager had called her the two days later, stating that something larger on an upper floor had just become available if she would be interested in that one for the same price.

"Is there something wrong with it?" she had questioned, wondering how she could be so lucky.

"Not at all. The owner's mother lived in the apartment for many years. He has only just become comfortable in having it rented now," the manager had explained. She hadn't hesitated for a second and accepted the new apartment sight unseen.

Dumping her lunch bag and purse on the beautiful entryway bench, Mia thanked whoever had moved out before her in such a hurry that they had left several beautifully carved pieces of furniture, a massive arched mirror, lamps, and even a few pictures. The manager had assured her she should use them.

After crossing the living area, she dropped into the office chair in front of her home computer. Staring at the black screen, Mia gathered her courage. She knew he was there—waiting for her to join him online. Rafael. The man she'd met on the fetish website.

The handsome, older man had sent a message within minutes when she'd introduced herself on the sub chat space. Using an alias to protect her identity, she'd gotten a lot of graphic messages that she'd immediately trashed. Rafael's message was different. She'd hesitated to respond, but something drew her to his direct message.

Your fantasies can come true. Let me show you how.

After reading and rereading his message, Mia had answered. His probing questions had demanded honesty, and she shared things she had told no one before. The older man mesmerized her. Taking advantage of every spare minute, Mia reached out to him over and over again online.

Soon Rafael knew her so well that it scared her and thrilled her at the same time. Mia hadn't ever told anyone about that secret need inside her. She had always been careful to keep it hidden away from everyone. Were there people like her out there? Those who needed… more from a relationship? Those who had the same dark desire.

She dragged herself through work and the drudgeries of life to steal those few minutes or hours talking with him online. He wasn't always there when she reached out to him. Irrationally, she was jealous of whatever or whoever, Mia thought with a jolt of anger, had captured his attention instead of her. She hadn't even met him. They weren't in a committed relationship. Mia just felt like she belonged with him.

Mia didn't understand it, but her heart beat faster each time he called her "my sweet." Something in him called to her, and she couldn't resist.

3

Pushing back from his computer, Rafael knew it was time to train Mia for her new role in his life. She responded eagerly to his guidance online. The anonymity of interacting through the chat room had allowed her to be honest and open about her fantasies. As he had suspected, she longed for the type of care he desired to lavish on his love. They were a perfect match.

He began plotting. A phone call to his ancestral home was at the top of his list. "Good morning, Anthony. Please begin preparations for me to return to the estate for an extended time. Expand the staff as needed to prepare for a guest in the downstairs residence as well as myself."

Smiling at the enthusiastic caretaker's response, Rafael knew Anthony understood his request completely. "Discretion should be the key factor in selecting staff, of course. I leave the decisions in your hands."

"It has been my pleasure to serve your family for many years. If you will forgive an old man's familiarity, I am glad that you have found her, sir."

"Thank you, Anthony."

"When can we expect your arrival?"

"Next week."

"Then I will get started today."

4

Arriving at her door on a Tuesday evening, Mia juggled the wet umbrella, her purse, and her lunch tote as she searched for her keys. She paused and looked around curiously. There was a scent lingering in the doorway. Her mind dismissed the fact that the aroma grew stronger as she leaned toward the door. Smelling of sandalwood, the cologne captured her attention as she inhaled. It was masculine and virile.

Shaking the silliness out of her head, Mia thrust her key into the lock and opened the door. She stepped inside and dropped everything onto the bench next to the door. Turning back to face into the apartment, she froze in place as something white caught her attention on the fashionable gray carpet.

An engraved invitation lay on the floor right inside the door. Just as if someone had stepped into her apartment and placed the crisp white envelope on the floor where she couldn't help but find it. She sniffed automatically. Her nose reacted once again to that scent that had tantalized her in the hallway. *He came in here!* The thought had her heart rate quickening.

Snatching her umbrella from the tumbled pile of belongings as a weapon, Mia raced through the apartment searching in every possible hiding spot for an intruder who had invaded her home. Nothing. Nothing was missing. Nothing was out of place. No one was there.

Slowly, she returned to the entryway to stare at that white envelope. Gathering her bravery around her like an impermeable cloak, she leaned over to pick it up with two fingers. That now familiar scent wafted up to her. "Okay! I'm really weirded out!" she muttered aloud to herself.

Mia turned and carried the envelope to the kitchen table where she dropped it. The impact slightly crumpled one corner. Instantly, she regretted the imperfection, and her fingers pressed the envelope as straight as possible. Once she touched it, she couldn't resist. Opening it carefully so as not to wrinkle or tear the thick paper again, Mia pulled out a single note card with one word written in a bold masculine script —*SOON*!

FOR THE NEXT THREE DAYS, Mia tried to forget the card and not think about what it meant. To distract herself, she tried to busy herself with work and connecting with friends. Mia shared her plans to go on vacation next week and that she was planning to take time away from all the electronics that ruled her life. Her home laptop would remain turned off and waiting on her desk.

Mia had won the reservations at the swanky resort escape through a drawing. She couldn't remember entering, but she always purchased raffle tickets from all her coworkers with children. Suspicious that this could be a scam, she'd researched the resort and contacted them directly to confirm everything. It was just what she needed. A getaway that promised no electronics or connections with the outside world. A place to recharge and just enjoy the beautiful area.

BLINKING into the predawn darkness on the first Saturday morning of her time off, Mia groaned. She lifted a pillow and dropped it over her eyes in disgust. She was now on vacation and she couldn't even sleep in. A ding rang out from her office in the quiet of the morning, reaching her ears even through the muffling pillow.

Confused by sleep and the early hour, she rolled out of bed and stumbled toward the sound. Blinking at the bright computer screen that had somehow turned on, Mia walked forward to see a message flashing on the screen from Rafael Montalvo. She clicked on it without a second thought.

There was only one question in the message: *Do you want your fantasies to come true?* A yes and no button followed. Nothing else.

Her finger crept forward to hesitate over the safe answer—no. She almost pressed it. In a burst of daring, Mia quickly tapped yes on the touch screen. A whisper of a sound behind her warned her something was off a fraction of a second before she felt the needle prick on the side of her neck. Struggling for only a few brief moments before her eyes rolled back in her head, Mia's body began to crumple toward the carpet. She did not reach the floor.

5

His fingers gently caressed the side of her face. With no makeup and her face relaxed into the induced slumber, Mia was exquisite. "My sweet, I have waited for you to appear for years. It's time for your training to begin."

Sweeping her up in his arms, Rafael placed her on the blanket he had stretched over the couch in the adjacent room. As he carefully enveloped her in the soft fabric, he looked around the décor of the familiar apartment. Mia had stamped her own personality here. So very different from his beloved mother's choices, Rafael knew that his parents would have loved Mia's flair.

Rafael took time to power off her phone and disconnect her computer before tucking her slim planner into the back of his waistband. Once cradled back in his arms, Mia automatically nestled into the curve of his throat. The trip down the private elevator took moments. With his precious bundle tucked into the back seat of his car, Rafael eased from his parking spot. Merging into traffic, he began the relatively brief trip out of the city to his family home.

He monitored his passenger easily from the video app playing on the display screen on his dash. The medication guaranteed her sleep for the journey, but he needed to see her. Rafael had waited too long to find Mia.

6

Waking in the absolute darkness, Mia stiffened in place. She'd never liked the dark. Even when she had been a little girl, she had slept with a nightlight. The ribbing she had gotten in her college dorm had been endless, but it had been better than the dark.

To keep herself from freaking out, Mia tried using all her senses to figure out where she was. She knew this wasn't home. She was lying on a cold concrete floor, not the soft carpet of her apartment. Unable to stop her movement, she shivered as the frigid temperature of the hard surface below her seeped into her bones. The oversized sleeveless nightshirt that she slept in did not ward off the cold.

Mia's head swiveled as she looked in all directions. When she couldn't distinguish anything, her hands began to twist nervously against her chest. *I don't like the dark. I don't like the dark. I don't like the dark*, repeated in her brain.

As if answering her plea for light, a bright spotlight illuminated a mattress three feet away from her. Her eyes locked upon it, and the light flashed off, leaving her in darkness once again. With spots before her eyes, Mia pushed her hands against the concrete floor to sit up.

As if the lack of light had activated her other senses, Mia automatically inhaled. There was a faint whiff of that elusive cologne she had smelled at her doorway. Chasing the scent, she sniffed the shoulder of her nightshirt. Yes! It was there! She pulled the center of her shirt to her nose. The smell was strong. She had been pressed against whoever wore that scent.

Mind reeling, she jumped as the spotlight again flashed on to the bare mattress for a few scant seconds before extinguishing once again. A deep voice spoke behind her, "Go, my sweet."

In a panic, she followed his directions and scrambled from her spot to the mattress. Her instincts processed the instruction before her mind recognized the actual words. *My sweet.* Pulling her legs in close to her body, Mia wrapped her arms around her shins. She pulled the bottom of her shirt over her knees to hide her body, cursing her habit of never wearing panties to bed. "Rafael, is that you? Why am I here?" Then, when there was no response, she whispered, "Are you going to hurt me?"

Silence echoed through the darkness. The young brunette's blue eyes searched desperately to see anything. Tense and scared, she replayed the fantasies she had shared with Rafael. Those that had her submit to him—to lose all control. Finally dropping her head to her knees in exhaustion, she dozed.

Her dreams were filled with that sandalwood cologne. A shadowy figure was always just out of sight. Even in her dreams, she whispered his name, "Rafael" as the fantasies she'd shared with that charismatic man seemed to come to life.

"It is time to wake up, my sweet," that deep voice whispered to her.

Waking to find herself still in the pitch-black room, Mia pinched herself to make sure she was really awake. That this wasn't a dream she needed to wake up from.

"Rafael? Could you let me go? I'm sorry I wasted your time," Mia asked quickly. "I made all that stuff up. I shouldn't have talked to you online."

"That is your first lie to me, Mia. Each time you lie, there will be a consequence. For this first lie, I will take your clothing. Pull off your shirt and throw it to me," Rafael answered evenly.

"I'm not wearing anything else. I can't take off my clothes. I don't know you," she refused with panic sounding in her voice. Her eyes searched the darkness in front of her.

"Your nightshirt, Mia." His voice was flat and adamant. "As this is the first time we have talked about the rules, I will offer you something in return. When your shirt is off, I will give you a light in exchange."

Mia shook her head frantically. "I'm not giving you my nightshirt."

"As you wish." The last sounds faded into the darkness.

Sitting there, her ears strained to hear anything in the obscurity. Nothing. "Rafael?" she asked hesitantly. No one answered.

She'd had enough. This man was playing a game with her she didn't like. He'd coaxed out of her all her fantasies of being owned or kept despite her attempts to conceal them. Now, he was using her own words against her. Wrapping her indignation around her slender frame, Mia pushed herself to the edge of the bare mattress and stood.

Waving her arms around in front of her, Mia tried to feel her way forward. After several steps, she looked behind her, and the mattress was no longer visible. Would she be able to find her way back? Mia began counting steps. *One, two, three.* When she reached twenty, she waved her hands around in a panic. How could there be nothing ahead of her? How big was this room he had trapped her in?

One fingertip on a flailing hand struck something hard with a dull ringing sound as she leaned forward. Stepping closer, her fingers wrapped around a cold metal bar. She slid her hand upward and even lifted onto her tiptoes. There was no end. Squatting quickly, she ran her hand down the metal to the cold concrete floor.

Shivering, she paused as her mind calculated. She reached to the left and found another bar and a column of bars followed out of her reach. Running her fingertips along the metal rods to the right, Mia's mind finally put the pieces together.

A cage. Rafael had locked her in a cage. Unable to stop herself, Mia pressed her knees together. Heat began to build in her lower abdomen. Pressing her thighs together, she tried to convince herself that she wasn't aroused. The wetness between her thighs betrayed her. This was the fantasy she had dreamed of for more years than she could recall.

She was trapped here at his mercy. The darkness wrapped around her as her hands clung to the iron bars. Would he remember all the wicked things that she had shared with him? Mia thought with a gasp. She turned around in the darkness, putting her back against the bars as her heart beat furiously in her chest and holding on to the bars for stability.

That scent of sandalwood whispered across her senses. Too late to whirl to face him, Mia felt the wide leather band wrap around her throat. It firmly pulled her head back against the bars and held her pinned there. Lunging forward, Mia choked herself, and as she struggled to breathe, she pressed back once again to feel the cold bars at her back. Her desperate attempts to free herself by striking behind her body only panicked Mia as she cut off her oxygen. Panting, she subsided against the bars of the cage that trapped her.

"That's much better, Mia. You will need to learn that I only ask once. If you do not comply, there will be a consequence," the deep voice came from behind her.

She felt the wide band at her throat jostle slightly. *Maybe it's loose!* Seizing her chance, she flung herself forward only to hit the unyielding restraint of the band. The force of her momentum brought tears and shimmering spots to her eyes. Choking, she fell back against the bars, clawing at the leather strip secured tightly around her throat and two bars behind her.

"You are behaving very badly, Mia. I think you will have punishment as well as your consequence." The low voice didn't alter. It was not angry, only matter-of-fact.

As she tried to breathe, Mia's brain registered that he could be remarking on the weather or the price of bananas at the store. Somehow, this lack of emotion scared her more. *Who is this man?*

A snip sounded very loudly behind her before the sound of shears or scissors opening and closing just once echoed in her ears. "You were told to take off your shirt. You did not choose to follow directions," the voice whispered, intimately close.

Trembling, Mia felt him pull the hem of the oversized shirt away from the back of her thighs. Lurching forward automatically, she subsided, gasping for air against the bars as that unyielding leather band held her firmly in place. Over her panting breath, she could hear the scissors slicing through the enveloping fabric of her nightshirt. Cold air wafted against the bare skin of her back and hips as he sliced up through the soft material. With a louder snip, he cut through the reinforced neckline.

Her mind raced to come up with a plan as he paused for a few seconds. *The shirt's still on my body. If he tries to cut anything else, he will be in reach this time.* Prepared to fight, a small sound of protest escaped from her mouth as he carefully snipped fabric across her shoulder blades in each direction. Her neck was held tight against the iron bars; twisting or turning would cut off her breath. If her arms couldn't reach him, he could do whatever he wanted.

She listened to each slow snip as he took his time cutting off the material that covered her upper back in each direction, destroying each slender strap that looped over her shoulders. Her hands held the soft cloth to her chest as it loosened around her body in a desperate attempt to stay covered. Mia shivered as she realized that she was helpless and he was in total control.

"Please, please don't do this," she finally begged as he reached the edge of the second strap.

At the clatter of the scissors falling behind her to the left, her head turned slightly to that side. In a flash, he jerked the destroyed shirt from behind to the right and through the bars.

"Aaah!" Mia screamed and crossed her arms quickly over her breasts as the cold air wrapped around her body. "Why are you doing this?" she demanded with hot tears of fright and frustration spilling from her eyes.

Silence was the only answer. Shrouded in darkness, she trembled against the bars, waiting to see what his next move would be. She heard a whisper of movement over to the left. Mia turned her head as much as possible, but she couldn't see anything. *Has he gone away?*

That deep voice finally answered from behind her, "You are here because you sought to fulfill your fantasies. Your heart is beating fast for two reasons: There is the fright, but most of all, you yearn. Do you recognize this from our conversations online? Do you remember what comes next?"

"Y… es," she forced from her mouth. Slowly, her hands slid from shielding her breasts down her torso. Their slow movement never faltered as the internal battle between her desire and her fear fought for control of her slender frame. Finally, her hands reached behind her body to latch on to the cold, metal bars.

A warm hand covered each of hers before she could panic and snatch them away. "Excellent, Mia. I knew you would remember," he praised her. "There's no one here but you and me. No one can hear us or watch us, just like in our conversations online. Didn't you wish we were together then?" His tone invited her to be a conspirator.

She tried to nod, forgetting about the restraint around her neck. "Yes. I was so excited about our upcoming date. I wanted to meet you," she confessed. Somehow it was easier in the dark to be truthful.

"Did you want me to touch you?" he asked.

He was so close. She could feel his warm breath on the top of her head. Mia squeezed her inner thighs together tightly, feeling the hot arousal fluid that coated them. She craved his touch. This man who was known to her but yet a stranger. Mia bit her lip as she fought her innate shyness that had always gotten in the way of any intimate relationship she could have enjoyed. She wanted to answer, but she couldn't.

"Would you like me to answer for you, Mia?" he asked in a patient tone that conveyed his understanding of her inability to say the word.

"Please?" she whispered.

His hands left hers. She continued to grip the bars as his warm hands traced along the outside of her arms, over the stressed muscles to her hunched shoulders. One masculine palm lifted from her torso to wrap around her throat over the leather band that secured her. His fingers tightened, scaring her for a few seconds before they released.

Rising to cradle her jaw, his thumb rubbed softly across her lips. "I am delighted that you are here, my sweet."

She tried to nod and winced as the leather bit into her neck.

"Soon, the band will not be necessary. You will learn that there are advantages to following my directions immediately."

As those ominous words echoed into the darkness, his fingertips lowered to trace down the midline of her body. Pausing between her uplifted breasts, his thumb brushed the sensitive swell underneath each small mound before continuing downward. That fleeting touch burned with intensity, making her gasp before her breath paused, waiting for his hand to reach its next target.

"Mia, did you follow my directions immediately?" he whispered into her ear.

So totally focused on the path of that hand, his words didn't process through her mind. His palm pressed against her slightly rounded lower belly before his fingers slid through the silky hair guarding her most private area. She bit her lip, wanting his touch so badly.

Her slender form jumped as his voice repeated the question louder, "Mia, did you follow my directions immediately?"

"What?" she asked distractedly, willing his fingers to move just a bit lower. When his hand followed her wishes, she gasped as he cupped the heat between her thighs and flexed his fingers to squeeze the soaked folds that betrayed her arousal.

That deep voice posed the question for the third time, "Did you follow my directions immediately, Mia?"

"N-no!" she stuttered, not understanding why his fingers didn't move. She needed him to touch her. "Please?" she begged.

To her dismay, that hand lifted from her body. "Wait!" The word burst from her lips before she could stop it. Unable to process what was happening, she felt something loop around each wrist and then pull them off the bars they clung to as a wide leather band was fastened around her waist.

Automatically, she pulled against the bonds that held her arms close to her torso. And then again because she couldn't process what was happening. Why wasn't he touching her? The band around her throat loosened and fell almost silently to the concrete below her bare feet. Mia heard his footsteps back away.

"This is your punishment, my sweet. Next time do as I ask instantly and you shall get your reward. Go to sleep." The spotlight flashed on, almost blinding her with its brightness. When she turned around to search the darkness beyond the bars, she knew that he was gone even though her blue eyes couldn't see anything beyond the bars.

Turning around to the light, she stumbled toward the lighted mattress. Mia pulled at the restraints around her waist that barred her hands from moving up or down her body. Just as she reached the padded surface, the light extinguished. Mia dropped to her knees and turned to sit with her back against the wall.

Clenching her knees together, she moaned in frustration, unable to touch herself or ease the heat that he had provoked. No matter how she turned or twisted, he had ensured that she would not be able to satisfy the burning need. Finally, her head dropped to her knees, and she escaped into sleep, promising herself that she would do as he asked immediately next time.

C rossing the familiar path out of the darkness, Rafael smiled at the many memories of coming to play here. He and his brother had often snuck into the lower level to explore, their desires to test their bravery as well as be close to the woman who had frequently inhabited the area where Mia now slept.

The dark allowed one to be their true self. Mia had delighted him with her dreams of containment and desire to experience the concealment that darkness offered. Her struggles to allow herself to live her fantasy would be easier without the harshness of light.

He lifted his fingers to his nostrils. Her scent clung to them, filling his senses with her sweet arousal. Thanks only to his rigid strength of will, Rafael had doled out her consequence and punishment without being distracted by her lovely form and sweet pleas for release.

Shifting his rigid shaft in his pants with his free hand, he paused at the stairs to listen as she tested her bonds. Her restlessness revealed her frustration. She would need to learn that her pleasure came only from him.

Her inhibitions would conflict with her desires for a short time. The darkness would allow her to submit fully to him. There, she could reveal her inner needs. Hearing her last sigh of acceptance, Rafael stroked himself one final time, denying his satisfaction as well. She would be worth the wait.

E yes blinking into the darkness, Mia wondered whether it was day or night. Unbelievably, she felt as if she had slept well. The coolness of the area that she was held in had eased, and even her bare skin was comfortable. Rolling her shoulders and using her elbow for leverage, Mia pushed herself back up to sit. At some point during her exhausted slumber, she had curled onto her side.

Her muscles were tight. Mia stood and rotated her hands to the front and the back of the waistband, locating the small lock that held it together. She rose onto her toes to stretch her legs. Then, dropping her heels to the ground, Mia leaned over to ease her back. Rising again to stand up, she leaned to the right and to the left before straightening.

Mia's body felt better. In her mind, she knew intrinsically that she was not in mortal danger. Rafael Montalvo would not kill her. She also knew from their conversations that he would make her suffer if she did not follow his wishes.

A whisper of sound alerted her he was near before a delicious smell reached her nose. Her stomach growled in reaction, making her wonder how long it had been since she had last eaten. A light bloomed to her right, making her blink as she tried to focus. Finally, a table set for breakfast and the seated handsome man who beckoned her forward with one hand solidified in front of her.

Without conscious thought, her feet jolted forward, eagerness rendering her movement ungraceful. Ordinarily, she would have slowed to regain her composure, but here, she knew that didn't matter. She wanted him to know her real self. Not the fake one she allowed others to see.

The other chair remained pushed in at the table, making her hesitate. Bewildered, she looked at him for a clue to tell her what to do.

"Come to me, my sweet," Rafael said, again lifting his hand to her. As Mia approached, his fingers wrapped around her waist and gently pulled her to stand between his legs. "Good morning, Mia," he greeted her warmly.

She stood rock still, suddenly painfully aware of her nudity. Feeling her body heating, she knew she was blushing as her hands attempted to lift to cover herself. Her movements shackled by the restraints around her waist, Mia hunched her shoulders to shield herself from his eyes.

"Never hide from me, Mia. Stand up straight. Present yourself to me," he commanded. Those dark eyes held hers, not allowing her to look away or refuse. He smiled as her shoulders eased back, the movement lifting her small breasts. "Very good, my sweet."

She could almost feel his eyes touching her as they glided from her face to her long neck over her breasts, torso, that sparse patch of silky hair that he had touched last night, and down her slender legs to the pink toenails decorated with white flowers for the beach vacation that she had planned. Rotating as the controlling hands at her waist turned her body, Mia tried not to shiver as she felt those dark eyes tracing over her back, hips, and legs.

Smack! A sharp swat to her right buttock rang out in the quiet room. His fingers looped into the leather band at her waist to halt her instinctive bolt forward as she gasped at the blooming pain. When she stilled, one finger traced the smarting area on her bottom. In her mind, Mia could see him caressing the border of a red handprint on her tender skin. She shivered.

"Your skin marks beautifully, my sweet. Just as I had expected. I will look forward to seeing your skin crisscrossed with the signs of our passion," Rafael murmured as he turned her around to face him once again.

His long, masculine fingers easily unfastened the restraints. Had she been watching closely, Mia would have seen that his large signet ring served as the key for the small locks. She was, however, distracted from his actions.

The young woman tried to memorize everything about Rafael. His dark hair was peppered with silver. Mia had already known that he was older. Fit with no extra padding, Rafael could have passed for a younger man without those silvery accents that hinted at his life experience. She liked that he did not hide the truth behind coloring carefully applied from a bottle. His handsome face drew her away from thoughts of age.

Devastatingly good-looking, Rafael's features were perfectly formed. Her blue eyes traced the firm line of his lips. Now relaxed as his fingers unfastened the final locks of the restraints, Mia suspected that the shape of his mouth would reveal his inner state—as would those dark eyes that captivated her. She could see the inner fire and passion that he held banked inside those mesmerizing orbs. Inhaling with delight, she smiled at the scent of sandalwood that had heralded his appearance each time.

"You are pleased this morning?" Rafael asked with curiosity.

"Is it morning?" she asked, trying to cover her reaction. Someone held captive shouldn't smile, should they?

"It is time for breakfast," he answered without truly answering. Standing, his toned body forced Mia to stumble back a few steps as he moved to pull her chair out for her. "Sit. Eat. You will need your energy."

Ravenous, she dropped into her seat. Mia picked up her fork and shoveled the first bite of the deliciously golden french toast into her mouth. He had prepared it just as she liked it with powdered sugar dusted on top instead of sticky syrup that overwhelmed the flavor.

Only when she had eaten the first piece did Mia notice that he was not eating with her.

Self-consciously, she set her fork down on her plate. "Aren't you hungry?" she asked, dragging her blue eyes from the remaining two pieces of toast on her plate.

"Eat, my sweet. You need to have the energy necessary to face the day." His voice was light, but she sensed something underneath.

Mia wanted to ask him what was coming, but one look at his handsome face revealed that she was not to ask. Quickly, she ate the remaining pieces of french toast on her plate. Sitting back, she patted her stomach. The feel of her own bare skin reminded her with a jolt she was naked in front of a fully clothed man.

Steeling herself not to cover her exposed flesh, Mia tried to remember what he was teaching her to do and not to do. Her eyes met his, and she watched him smile slightly. She knew that he had been watching her as she struggled mentally to behave as he desired.

"Very good, my sweet. You are learning. Now it is time for you to return to your mat. This will be your last free meal in my home. You will earn the right to sit at my table from now on," he warned.

"What…" she began to ask, only stopping when his hand came up to signal her to stop.

"Your mat," he repeated, pointing to the spotlighted mattress on the floor.

Standing, Mia walked a few steps away before turning to look back at the table. The area was now all shadowed by the enveloping darkness. Mia shivered. Suddenly, the entire area felt abandoned. The charismatic Rafael Montalvo was gone. Unable to stop herself, Mia ran to the familiar mattress and sat quickly on top of it just as the light blinked out, leaving her again in total darkness.

9

A short time later, a whisper of movement caught her attention. Mia called into the surrounding blackness, "Rafael? Is that you?"

No one answered. The slight sound of someone's clothing rustling as they moved was the only sound that she heard before the squeak of wheels. That metallic sound pierced the quiet area, magnifying its loudness.

"Who's there? I need to get..." A loud buzzing sound disrupted her words. The sound continued for several minutes before cutting off suddenly. Mia's ears reverberated from the effects of the loud sound.

"Are you still there?" she called into the room she already expected was now empty.

Darkness and silence surrounded her. Idle for the first time in years, Mia craved the mindless escape that her cell phone or tablet would give her. Here, isolated from everything, she had no distractions from her thoughts. No fake friends to try to impress with her latest meal. Nothing.

Mia's mind raced. Would anyone notice her disappearance? Would anyone care? Surely that person who had whisked everything from the table would alert the authorities that Rafael held someone in the dark.

A sinking feeling dropped over her. She stretched out on the mattress with her hands pressed against her full stomach. No one would sound the alarm. That employee wouldn't report his or her boss.

Her vacation would cover her disappearance from her personal life. Her plane ticket would go unused, and the airline would fill her empty seat with one of the hopeful standby passengers. At work, her empty cubicle wouldn't alarm anyone. If anyone even noticed she was missing, her request taped to her office chair asking others not to steal it while she was on vacation would delay questions about her whereabouts. Without close family or even friends, she realized that she could be gone for a long time before anyone noticed.

"What a sad life I have," she whispered into the darkness as she realized that no one would really care if she didn't show back up. Her fingers caressed her slightly swollen belly. He'd fed her. Even held captive here in the darkness, Rafael Montalvo had already acknowledged her existence more than those who saw her every day.

Quiet, sad tears rolled over her cheeks to land on the soft padding of the mattress below her. Her life lacked sparks, excitement… love. Mia's eyes closed, exhausted by the soul searching that had consumed her thoughts.

THE MAN who watched noted her breath evening out as the enticing young woman he had found online escaped into sleep. He smiled behind the bank of monitors showing her activities clearly even in the dark. Upon finding her, Rafael had modernized this area carefully. Money had not been a concern.

Designed by his father during the construction of the mansion, the bars and other features were permanent features of the large home. The elder Montalvo had used this layout throughout his life with the woman he had claimed. Their marriage lasted for fifty-six years and resulted in three children.

Sarah, the eldest daughter, married at twenty-three. The son of the elder Montalvo's partner chose her when she was eighteen. When finished with her schooling, Sarah had returned home eagerly. She was suited to the lifestyle and adored her powerful husband, even when the consequences of her transgressions challenged her.

Rafael saw her from time to time. Her husband had assisted Rafael in updating the old structure. Advances in technology enhanced it now. Mia was cloaked in darkness to allow her to learn how to be the woman who lurked inside her. But Rafael could oversee the process closely. He would not risk any damage coming to her.

Emotion battled inside him. He could see her clearly as she cried. This was the first step for the young woman. Realizing the cold, sad facts of her current life would help her transition away from everything that she had become accustomed. Shedding the artificial trappings of modern life, Mia would blossom in this more suitable way of life for her. She had no idea of the extent of his plans. His Mia was simply perfect.

10

The sound of something grating across the floor woke Mia from a deep sleep. She scrambled to her knees on the mattress, trying desperately to see through the darkness. The rasping sound continued. From the sound alone, she could tell that it was large and heavy.

When it stopped, Mia called out, "Rafael? Is that you?"

Silence answered her question. Several long moments followed as she hovered in place, unsure about what to do. A sudden burst of light drew her attention to a padded bench. Torn between her curiosity and her sudden unease, Mia rose to her feet but remained poised by her mat. Seconds passed before she took one tentative step forward.

As her bare foot touched the ground, Rafael appeared next to the bench. "Come, my sweet," he commanded. There was no other description of his tone. His voice was definite and demanding.

As if drawn to him by an invisible rope, Mia took small steps toward him. Many times, she almost turned to flee back to the refuge her mattress offered, but his eyes held hers, not allowing her to run away. Finally, she stepped into the circle of light.

"Very good, my sweet. You are learning well," his voice complimented as Rafael extended a hand to her.

Unable to resist, Mia placed her hand upon his warm palm.

Allowing herself to be drawn forward, she yielded to the pressure his left hand placed on her shoulder, and she knelt on the padded lower platform. The young woman looked over her shoulder at the man leaning over her now to ask, "What is this?" Her voice trembled with fright.

"This is where you let go of your past and begin again," he answered quietly. Rafael's hand left hers to join the other on her shoulder. His strength pressed her firmly onto the padded bench that stretched in two sections before her, only allowing her breasts to hang freely in the empty space between the supports. Once in position, he quickly secured her with a thick leather restraint around her waist.

"Rafael, I don't like this. I'm scared! Let me go, please?" Mia begged.

The handsome man moved with a quiet grace to stand at the front of the device. "Give me your hands, my sweet," he requested as if she hadn't spoken.

To her horror, she followed his directions and reached her hands forward to him. Quickly, he wrapped restraints around her wrists, tethering them below her head. Mia's eyes focused on the special curved pad in front of her. Her neck stiffened as his hand pressed her head down onto that support. Carefully he adjusted its position before one heavy hand threaded through her tangled brown hair to hold her forehead down to the mat as he tightened the last restraint, a web of strips cupping the back of her head.

She struggled on the bench, unable to keep herself from testing the strength of the bonds that held her in position. Mia's pleas for him to release her echoed unanswered in the silent room. Her breath came in pants as she exhausted her energy.

When she finally went limp in this position, his hands caressed over her head, shoulders and back to cup her bottom. His touch drew her attention to the heat that had built between her thighs. Mia's eyes closed as she realized that her body was aroused by the bonds, just like she had responded when pinned against the bars. Pressing back toward his hands, she silently urged him to touch her more intimately.

Rafael's deep voice answered her this time. "I know, my sweet. I know what you crave." His hands lifted from her bottom.

Mia felt his body heat step away. Unable to turn her head to see what was happening anywhere but for the small space under the curved resting pad, the young woman held her breath as she tried to hear what was happening. A faint rustling came from behind her body before a flare of pain burst over her.

"What's that?" she asked in a panicked voice. It felt as if it had taken a hundred little bites out of her skin. His warm hand soothing over her skin calmed her slightly. There was no stickiness or fluid. She wasn't bleeding.

"Your skin marks beautifully, my sweet. Embrace the pain," he recommended.

Again and again, the strips of the flogger lashed against her skin. Mia writhed against the leather, her movements limited severely by the restraints. Only her breasts were allowed to move freely in response to the blows. Tears dropped from her eyes to land on the concrete floor below her. The pain began to blur together as the steady rain of blows streamed over her skin.

Each blow to her back and bottom transported her to a place where pain and pleasure blended together. All thoughts were erased from Mia's mind as the points of pain ruled her senses. Her mind began to float inside her head. The impact of the flogger swept her body into a trancelike enjoyment of the sensations. She could think of nothing else but the sting of the flogger and the caress of his warm hand on her skin.

Mia was unaware of when the flogging stopped. She could only concentrate on the feel of his smooth hand, worshipping her punished skin with silky caresses. His fingers touched her everywhere, pulling soft moans of enjoyment from her open mouth. Rafael's gentle tug on her hair, his fingers tightly rolling her nipples, the massaging contact on her back all flowed together with the stinging pain.

"Please, Rafael," she begged, repeatedly, not even knowing what she was asking him for.

"Shhh, my sweet. I will take care of you," he promised as one hand drifted over the curve of her bottom to trace her slick outer lips.

Had she been able to see his face, Mia would have blushed at the heat and desire etched into his handsome features. Tightly bound in place, her mind swam with pleasure as his fingers delved into her intimate folds. The young woman moaned at his touch as he traced the entrance to her vagina. He pinched her clitoris sharply, and Mia moaned as he continued to weave together pain and pleasure. Like a junkie, she was becoming obsessed with the fine line between them.

Slick with her juices, Rafael's long finger entered her body. Keening in pleasure, Mia begged, "Faster, please, Rafael!" To her frustration, his speed didn't alter. She was not in charge. At his whim, Rafael could please her or not.

"Breathe, my sweet," he ordered.

Air gushed from Mia's lips when she realized she held her breath. Her inhale filled her nostrils with the sweet smell of her desire. She craved his touch. "Please, Rafael. Don't punish me. I need your touch. I need this."

"You will earn my touches soon by pleasing me. Would you like to please me, my sweet?"

"Yes!"

His finger continued its slow path in and out of her. She strained forward and back the miniscule amount that she could, so concentrated on his caresses that she almost missed his words.

"You are learning so fast, Mia. I knew immediately that you were the one I've been searching for. The one who needed the dark and my touch."

"Please!" she begged. Her entire focus centered on that slow-moving invader.

"I think you've earned a reward. You'll remember to follow directions in the future, won't you, my sweet."

"Yes, Rafael!" She would have promised him anything as his finger became two and he rotated his hand to brush that engorged bundle of nerves with his thumb.

Slowly, he increased the speed and the depth of his thrusts. "Close your eyes, Mia. Shut out the light," he instructed.

Obediently, she squeezed her lashes together. She could feel her body nearing a climax. Totally concentrating on the sensations between her legs, Mia writhed on the supportive bench behind her. *Smack!* A sudden swat of his hand on her bottom drew her attention back to her stinging skin. The whirling sensations pushed her arousal higher. Within seconds his skillful caresses launched her into a massive orgasm.

Struggling to survive the pleasure that cascaded over her, Mia was unaware that his adoring touches to her body also heralded her release from her bonds. Unwilling to leave this bench that had brought her gratification unlike any she'd ever felt, her fingers clutched to the padded rests as he lifted her away. Only when cradled against his muscular body did she willingly leave its sensual support. Looping her arms around his neck, Mia held fast to Rafael.

"You did well, my sweet. I will look forward to bringing you pain and pleasure again," he complimented her warmly. When Mia offered her lips to Rafael, he simply traced the outline of her pink mouth before smoothing her hair back and tucking it behind her ear. "Soon, my sweet," he promised. "Soon, you will earn the privilege."

Mia didn't know how long Rafael held her in his arms. Cradled against his hard body, he was in control, making her drink water as he spoke softly to her. When she began to emerge from the subspace that the flogging had transported her to, the handsome man smoothed a soothing cream over the reddened flesh on her back and buttocks before carrying her to the sanctuary of her mat. His footsteps were sure as he walked from the circle of light that spotlighted the padded bench into the darkness.

Mia protested leaving his arms when he laid her softly on the mattress. Her fingers clung to his shirt, unwilling to lose his touch. His fingers firmly unhooked her hold without comment or reassurance. She relented reluctantly, unable to prevent the soft protesting whimpers from welling through her lips.

Those small sounds continued as he walked away and only ceased when he returned to wrap her in a soft blanket. Then, wrapped in comfort and warmth, she succumbed to the absolute exhaustion that flooded her body and mind. Falling fast asleep, Mia missed seeing the light blink out of existence as darkness surrounded her once again.

D ragging himself away from the rumpled bundle lying on the mat, Rafael held his ironlike control together. He had waited for her too long to show weakness during her training. Her responses delighted him, proving he had chosen well. She was the one he had sought for many years.

He knew that she would challenge him. The spark inside her would require her to struggle. That inner fire needed to be carefully tended. It would help bond Mia to him completely.

Rafael knew she needed to resist him from time to time to enjoy the consequences. Her mind would not allow her to submit completely without his dominance. When he was in control, she could experience her deepest fantasies without the need to protest or run away to protect herself from what others would judge as wrong. Nothing would be off-limits in their relationship.

"I will give her all she desires and needs," Rafael promised aloud as he activated the cameras monitoring Mia. The spoken words sealed the mental contract that he had constructed over the years as he'd waited to find his one. Settling behind his desk, Rafael gave himself five minutes to watch her sleep. Rotating the heavy signet ring on his pinkie, he rubbed the raised surface on his leather blotter. The motion cleared the accumulated tarnish away, revealing a set of three letters: *KOD*.

Finally, he forced himself to concentrate on his business. Reviewing documentation for a merger, Rafael focused on the wording in the legal contract. Finding several questionable clauses, he made detailed notes and change requests. Alerted by the stealthy and misleading wording, he flagged it in the system for review by his most experienced and trusted lawyer in his firm.

Glancing back to the screen focused on the mattress several hours later, he discovered it was empty. Rafael felt his lips curve in a slow smile as he reached forward to activate the other cameras. After locating her, Rafael pushed back from his desk as he activated the timer on his watch. It was time for lunch. She would need to learn that wandering from his instructions had consequences. Any misbehavior would be severely punished.

12

R ubbing her cheek against the soft material, the corners of Mia's mouth curved in response to the scent of sandalwood that clung to the fabric. Her eyes blinked open to see the familiar blackness around her. Shifting slightly under the blanket, she groaned as she felt the stiffness that had spread across her back.

"Aaah!" she moaned as she pushed herself up to sit. Propping herself against the concrete wall, she sighed in relief as the smooth, cool surface soothed her abused skin. Closing her eyes, she replayed her last encounter with Rafael.

The pain of the flogging now blunted in her memory, she focused on his hands caressing her as she wantonly begged for his touch. Blushing as she remembered her pleas, Mia knew she had never wanted a release as much as after the flogging. But not by just anyone's touch. She had wanted Rafael's fingers to stroke her.

She shook her head, trying to understand how she could react so differently with Rafael than with the three other men she had been intimate with. They had not brought her the pleasure that she could create with her own fingers. She had simply faked orgasms when their touch left her unexcited.

Gazing out into the darkness, her mind tried to solve the puzzle of whether she was frigid or whether they were terrible lovers. The easy answer was that they did not have the experience that she needed. She searched for the real answer, but her mind skittered away from the truth.

With a shake of her head to stop her whirling thoughts, Mia pushed herself to the edge of the mattress and stood. She needed to do something. Pacing forward to explore, Mia counted her steps. At forty-two, her searching fingers brushed the iron bars. After a short mental debate, she turned to her left and followed the iron bars.

By the third turn of the bars, Mia was completely disoriented. Trailing her right hand against the bars as she walked to stay close to the barrier, she stopped in disbelief as her left shoulder touched a bar as well—another turn in the line of bars. Confused, she had expected to find herself in a square or rectangular area. Again, she turned to keep her right hand against the bars and took a step forward.

WHACK! Her forehead struck a horizontal bar. Only able to step back a few inches into the corner, Mia cried out in pain. Tears welled in her eyes as her fingers tentatively pressed against the tender spot and felt it beginning to swell. Her right hand struck out angrily at the bar she knew hadn't been there just a few seconds ago. Crying out in pain once again, she cradled her right hand to her breasts and tentatively held her left hand out. Now, there were three iron rods stretched in front of her face.

Beginning to panic, she bent her legs to duck under the barrier only to gasp in pain as her kneecaps struck more of the unyielding metal poles. Mia pressed her shin forward to discover an irregular arrangement of horizontal bars that prevented her from freeing herself from below. She was penned in a small triangular space.

Unable to turn around or move, she began desperately calling for Rafael. "What is this? Can you help me out? I don't understand. Why am I trapped here? Please, let me out."

Mia had no idea how long she called for help. Hours seemed to pass with no response from Rafael. Her voice grew hoarse and weak as her legs trembled from standing in the same place for so long. Feeling the knot swelling on her forehead, Mia's head began to throb. The young woman leaned forward and to each side to press against the bars, looking for any sign of weakness that she could take advantage of. They were rigid against her body.

When she'd almost lost hope that he would ever come to help her, her nose captured that distinctive scent. "Rafael?" she croaked virtually soundlessly.

"I am very disappointed in you, Mia."

His use of her name instead of his usual "my sweet" brought tears to her eyes. "I'm sorry," she pushed desperately from her abused throat.

"There is no escape from this place. It is futile to try. There are safeguards and traps to capture you if you dare to look for a way out," he informed her coldly.

The darkness shielded his face from her as he approached. *How does he see?* He moved through the shadows as if he had been born to them. He was now close enough for her to feel his warmth. She reached her hands as far as possible through the iron bars. Her fingertips were badly abraded and bruised from the frantic search to free herself from the cage around her. When her fingers on one hand brushed the back of his, they moved to cling to Rafael, needing to connect with him.

Coldly, his hand shook her grip away. Crushed, she leaned back into the corner, making herself as small as she could. Tears cascaded down her cheeks at the feeling of being more alone than ever. "I didn't try… to escape." Her voice cracked as she tried to explain.

There was no response other than a mechanical clicking that sounded in front of her. Mia realized that he was releasing the trap that had closed around her. She tried again. "I was just exploring. I'm sorry."

Mia felt the air around her move slightly, as if something had disturbed it. She cautiously extended her arms. The bars had vanished. Stepping forward eagerly, her overtaxed legs collapsed under her, and she fell ungracefully to her knees with a muffled sound of pain. "Rafael?" she whispered into the space she already knew was empty.

The light over the mattress flared again. Forcing herself to her feet, she stumbled to the padded mat. She couldn't believe it was so far away. No wonder Rafael believed she was trying to escape. Collapsing onto the oasis the simple cushion had become just as the lights again extinguished, Mia lay down. Her battered fingers searched for the blanket that she already knew would be gone. Defeated, she curled into a ball and closed her eyes, unable to cry anymore, the surrounding chill sinking into her bones.

13
---

wo steps forward and one backward. Rafael stowed the soft blanket away. She would have to earn it back now. Her forehead concerned him. He did not like to see his possessions damaged. That thought stopped him in his tracks. He already considered her his.

Instead of being disturbed by this idea, Rafael was pleased. Mia belonged to him now. Speaking to his housekeeper, he ordered her to gather a few items on a tray. It would need to be ready in two hours. She would sleep until then.

Returning to his office, Rafael immersed himself in paperwork. With Mia in his home, he would be unwilling to spend his normal long hours dealing with business. The need to be close to her grew inside him. Only discipline, forged from years of dedication to his financial interests, kept him from repeatedly checking on her prone body.

When his housekeeper knocked on the heavy, locked door to his home office, Rafael buzzed her inside. "Thank you, Margaret. Just set the tray on the table there. I will see to it in a moment."

With a deferential "Yes, sir," the housekeeper followed his directions and departed.

Ten minutes later, Rafael stood and stretched as he referred to his watch. It was time to check on Mia. Picking up the tray, Rafael approached his door and stopped a foot before reaching the heavy oak barrier. He made a quick detour to the jar of sweets in his office. Never touching the sugary treats, Rafael kept them there for business professionals invited for more private collaborations. It was always telling to see who bowed to the temptation.

Soon, he crossed the darkened floor silently. Entering the enclosed space, Rafael approached the mattress. Mia had curled into a protective ball. The lump on her forehead was pronounced. He would watch how easily she awoke and monitor her for a concussion. *Now that she's mine, I won't allow her to be harmed.*

Rafael paused as the impact of his words registered on his mind. Already, she was his. He couldn't let her go. She was too important.

Quietly, he arranged the supplies on the floor next to her sleeping form. As he placed one sweet treat on the ground, he tried to convince himself that her throat needed soothing to repair the damage of her calls to him for help. He would only leave one. He did not wish to spoil her. After all, she'd called for him.

She called for me. Another uncharacteristic smile curved his lips as he strode quietly from her side. *She called for me.*

14

That scent woke her. The one that heralded Rafael's presence. As quickly as her abused skin and stiff body could move, Mia pushed herself up.

"Rafael?" she asked, hopefully. Her voice was almost nonexistent. Mia's hand rose to cover her throat as if she could will her vocal cords to function.

Only the vanishing scent answered her. The young woman licked her cracking lips. It had been so long since she'd had anything to drink. That meal of golden french toast seemed like a thousand years ago. Mia slumped back onto one elbow and heard something fall over next to the edge of the mattress. Her battered fingers slid over the edge to search the floor.

"Oh, thank you!" she croaked as her hand closed over a large bottle of water. Eagerly, she sat up and rushed to twist off the plastic lid. Her desperate, huge gulps sloshed water from her lips.

Mia forced herself to slow down so she wouldn't waste a drop of the precious liquid. Her fingers scooped up the errant drops, carrying them to her mouth. When the bottle felt half-empty, she made herself screw the top back on. Holding it up to her forehead, she pressed the plastic container filled with cold water lightly against the large knot that throbbed incessantly. "Aaah!" she said as her headache eased a bit.

Mia lay back down on the soft surface and reached back to the ground to see if anything else just happened to be lying there as well. To her delight, she discovered two additional water bottles. Even better, as she settled back, her arm brushed a small ice pack and something little and round wrapped in a crinkly wrapper. Placing her hand on top of these new treasures to keep them close, Mia immediately sat up to chug the other half of the liquid in the bottle she had been hoarding.

Setting that empty plastic bottle carefully between her body and the wall so it couldn't get lost in the darkness, Mia rolled onto her back and placed the ice pack on her aching forehead. "Ohhh!" she sighed in delight at the cooling sensation. Actually, there wasn't any part of her that didn't feel as if it had escaped being run over by a speeding train.

Remembering the crinkling paper, she lifted the small object to her mouth and sniffed. Peppermint filled her nostrils. Eagerly, she ripped open the wrapper and shoved it in her mouth. "Mmmm," she hummed with happiness as the mint flavor filled her mouth and soothed her raw throat. Careful not to crunch down on the mint so she didn't eat it too quickly, Mia sucked on the candy, savoring it more than she'd ever enjoyed anything in her life.

Several minutes passed before she said as loudly as possible, "Thank you, Rafael. I'm sorry I disappointed you. I wasn't trying to run away. I was just exploring. Please forgive me." Her voice cracked at the end as her emotions swelled inside her chest.

"Please?"

Silence once again filled the darkened space. Mia had no idea how long she waited, hoping for an answer. A light flickered on and off to her left. Another followed a short distance away from the foot of her bed. Her head tilted back to see a light pulse on past the head of the mattress. Laughing with delight, Mia clapped her hands.

He'd heard her. He'd even brought her something sweet. Mia's heart lurched at that thought. My sweet. Was the candy a way of telling her he forgave her? Wrapping her arms around herself, Mia smiled for the first time in hours.

The ice pack was growing warm when Mia realized that she needed to go to the bathroom. *How long have I been here?* she wondered. It felt like two days, but this was the first time she'd needed to go. Maybe she hadn't been here that long. There was no denying that she needed to go now. *What am I supposed to do?*

She debated walking along the wall to a spot away from her mat and just peeing, but she was afraid that she'd be caught in a trap again. Finally, mortified to have to ask him, Mia called out, "Rafael? I don't know what to do. I need to go to the bathroom." The water and mint had soothed her hoarse voice slightly, but still, she worried that he wouldn't hear her.

There was no response. Finally, afraid that she would wet the mattress, Mia stood and took two steps away from her place of safety. She wrapped her arms around herself as she desperately squeezed her legs together.

"Come here, my sweet." She heard his voice behind her. "Walk to my voice," he asked.

Scrambling toward him, Mia froze for only a few seconds as a light flashed on above them. Her steps flew to the low camp toilet that sat next to him, and she frantically dropped to the seat. Mortified to be urinating in front of anyone, Mia hunched forward, and her hands flew up to cover her flaming face. To her amazement, he didn't walk away in disgust but moved closer until her hands touched the soft fabric of his pants.

Instinctively, she wrapped her arms around his legs to feel the human touch of his warmth against her face. He was here. He had come again. "Thank you, Rafael," she croaked. To her delight, his hand cupped the back of her head and held her close to his thighs.

"I will always come when you call, my sweet. You belong to me now."

Without pausing to question his words, she nodded. She belonged to him.

WHEN SHE HAD FINISHED, Rafael helped her clean up before moving the toilet to sit next to the wall. At his request, she practiced walking back and forth to the toilet from her mat. Six steps from the head of her mattress and she would run into it. She promised him she wouldn't forget.

Blinking in the white glare of the spotlight, Mia tried to memorize the features of the man in total control of her life. His hair was dark brown or black. She couldn't tell in this light. It sparkled with silver threads mixed throughout his elegantly styled hair. Dressed in an immaculate suit, Rafael Montalvo looked like he could have been standing in front of a board of directors in an exclusive company.

His formal dress made the young woman feel even more naked. His dark eyes surveyed her body possessively, causing Mia to feel less embarrassed by her exposure and strangely prouder of earning his interest. She straightened her posture to allow him to see her clearly. Her thoughts were a jumble that somehow resulted in her wishing that he would be pleased with her. She needed him to be attracted to her.

Rafael's fingers lifted her chin just slightly more. She realized that he was examining the knot on her forehead she had forgotten. The cool fingers of his other hand explored the swelling that remained. "You have learned that I alone can keep you safe and happy, my sweet. Have you learned any other lessons since you arrived here?"

"Oh, yes," Mia rushed to reassure him. "I know to follow directions immediately and to never wander away." She looked at him, hoping that her answer would be the one he wanted to hear. To her dismay, he continued looking at her as if there was something else that she needed to say. Thinking furiously, she remembered to add, "And... that you will always come when I need you."

"You have forgotten the most important part, my sweet," he said, shaking his head sadly.

"I'm sorry. I can't remember." Grasping at straws to avoid angering him, she added, "Perhaps I can't remember because I bumped my head. Can you help me remember?"

"You belong to me." The words were uttered singularly, with an equal emphasis placed on each one.

"Oh, yes. I belong to you while you keep me here," she rushed to repeat.

"No. You belong to me," he repeated.

Staring at him in the ring of whiteness created by the spotlight, Mia couldn't stop the shiver of reaction that flooded her body. Those words had featured strongly in her fantasies.

She wanted to belong to someone. Not like the love interest of a dedicated boyfriend or husband. When she admitted the truth even to herself, her secret dreams and desires focused on a strong man who ruled her.

She shivered under his knowing gaze. "But you don't really know me," she whispered.

"Don't I? I know if I touch your arm that you will feel my touch between your tightly clenched thighs."

He reached out and drew his fingers lightly down the side of her arm from shoulder to forearm. He paused, watching her closely as the muscles in her legs flexed. There were no secrets between them.

"If I do this," he said in the same matter-of-fact tone as his hand seized her wrist in a grip that immediately brought tears to her eyes. He spun her around to bend her arm up behind her before adding, "You're even wetter." His other hand slid over her reddened bottom to cup her labia.

"Aaah!" The gasp was forced from her lips by the surprise and his forceful and invasive touch. Mia dropped her head forward in shame as she felt herself gush against his warm hand.

He was right. *How is he right?*

When his heat loomed against her, her back straightened automatically. He was so close. Mia leaned back slightly over her captured hand pressed almost between her shoulders. She craved contact with his body. When the skin of her back touched the fine wool of his blazer, her eyes closed in enjoyment as she inhaled the sandalwood cologne that always lingered around him.

His head tilted forward to press a light kiss to that sensitive spot between her neck and shoulder. Rising away from her bare flesh only to return as if drawn back to this tender spot, Mia moaned as his mouth opened, this time to bite down firmly on the captured flesh. But for the hand cupped between her legs, Mia's knees would have buckled as his tongue lapped over the embedded teeth marks that remained imprinted in her flesh.

"Mine, Mia. You belong to me."

When his hands released her without another word, Mia collapsed to her knees on the padded mat. The light over her vanished. The whisper of his leather shoes on the concrete was the only clue that she was alone once again. She inhaled deeply to savor the dissipating scent of this man who knew her better than she knew herself.

Crawling fully onto the soft mattress, Mia curled into a ball. Closing her eyes, her hand rose to trace the small indentations from his white teeth in her flesh. He had staked his claim. Suddenly exhausted, she laid her hand over the marks and allowed herself to rest.

15

R afael's mind boggled at the depth of his desire as he forced himself to walk away. "No," he pressured himself to admit as he climbed the stairs, putting distance between them. Desire was not the only emotion he felt toward the slight brunette. The connection between them could not be denied.

He could have taken her then on the mat. She would have yielded to him without protest. But Rafael wanted more. He wanted everything from her. He could accept nothing less.

Rafael enjoyed a delicious meal before returning to his office to review the latest version of the deceptive contract. He had always spent long hours developing his business. Now, however, the work provided a needed distraction from the delight that huddled on the mattress.

When exhausted, he forced himself from his desk and climbed the stairs to his suite. Hanging the suit to be cleaned, Rafael stood at the end of his bed. It was time to have a mattress for Mia placed alongside. Her lessons would need to continue when she emerged from the darkness.

Striding into the large master bathroom, Rafael switched on the water in the shower to allow it to warm up as he brushed his teeth. Gazing in the mirror, he contemplated the silver strands in his hair.

There had been a number of women who he had chosen to be intimate with over the years. He had waited so long to find the perfect fit for his desires.

He pushed the fleeting thought that he wished he'd met Mia sooner from his head. All those shining strands attested to the journey that had brought him to this moment in time. Now was the perfect time to have her here. He would not waste time on silly thoughts. They would have many years together.

After rinsing his mouth, Rafael stepped into the warm spray. He closed his eyes in appreciation of the water cascading over him. Instantly, a vision of Mia leapt into his mind. His body responded immediately to the allure of her delicate curves. Wrapping his hand around his engorging shaft, Rafael pulled strongly from the thick base to the broad head. With a groan, he repeated the action over and over as he imagined what she could feel like wrapped around his cock. Rafael visualized how he would take her first. His erection jerked in his hand at the erotic images playing through his head. It did not take long for him to explode over the slate tiles.

Rafael finished his shower quickly before stepping out to towel himself roughly dry. Heading for his solitary bed, he thrust his hands through his hair to force it into the style he preferred. Unable to prevent himself, Rafael checked the video feed on his phone. Mia was safe and curled on her mattress.

He would give her some time to reflect on how important he was now in her life. She would need some processing time. With that decision made, Rafael closed his eyes. He could allow himself to sleep.

16

Huddling on the mattress, Mia's mind churned with anxious thoughts. She hadn't heard from Rafael for what seemed like days. Unable to track time, she'd counted the number of trips she'd made to the toilet. *Four.*

Thin fingers uncapped the last bottle of water that he had left for her. Mia took a small sip to wet her parched mouth and then forced herself to close it and set the plastic container aside. Regretting the sizeable amount of water that she had consumed in the beginning, she now rationed herself to small dribbles of the precious liquid.

Why has he abandoned me? she wondered. Scared by his blatant claiming of her and her traitorous body's reaction to his touch, Mia had stubbornly decided that she would not call for him.

Hungry, cold, and forsaken, Mia was forced to change her mind. "Rafael?" she tentatively called.

Almost instantly, a small light flickered on a few feet away from her. Hopeful, she called again. "Rafael? I need you. Can you help me? I'm almost out of water…" Her voice cracked with emotion. "I'm hungry."

When no further response happened, she whispered, "I belong to you. Won't you come care for me?"

His voice echoed through the chamber. It was projected through some sort of intercom system. "I am coming. Wait for me."

It seemed to take forever. Mia smelled it coming before she heard the catlike grace of his walk. Her stomach growled loudly. Before she could stop herself, she stood on the ground next to her mat. One heel pressed against the cushion to maintain her contact with her safe place as she leaned forward to sniff.

"Pizza?" she asked, her mouth already salivating at the smell of tomatoes and cheese.

"Leonardo's," he answered, drawing near.

"How did you…" Mia started to ask how he had known it was her favorite restaurant of all time but remembered all those topics they had discussed online. A thrill went through her that he had paid such attention to their small, meaningless conversation.

The light over her mat switched on as he drew closer. Without a second thought, Mia rushed forward to throw her arms around Rafael's waist. As he pulled her close, she closed her eyes to enjoy the feel of his warm body pressed to hers. Even the feeling of the pizza box bumping into her back didn't distract her from enjoying him. He was more important than any food could be.

"My sweet, let me feed you," he asked her when he finally stepped away from her. "Sit and we will eat," he suggested, toeing off his shoes and stepping onto her mat.

Delighted, Mia scrambled into her favorite position—back against the concrete. This time, she sat at one end of the mattress to allow him to sit down next to her. Hands clasped at her heart, she watched Rafael gracefully lower himself to the padded surface and place the box in the empty space before him. Only when his hands opened a fizzing can of soda and handed Mia the container did she realize that he had balanced a six-pack of soft drinks as well as the pizza.

Greedily guzzling the bubbly drink, Mia forced herself to stop drinking and lower the can. She smiled as he nodded approvingly before opening the top of the box. The rush of the steam from the box made her lean forward to inhale the heavenly aroma. Never had pizza smelled so good.

Rafael dropped a hand on her knee, keeping her from rushing to scoop up a piece. When she sat back slightly, he lifted his hand to reach into the box and carefully selected the largest piece of the pie and handed it to her. "Careful, my sweet. It is hot." When he encouraged her with a nod, Mia tentatively brought the piece to her lips and took a delicate, careful bite of the hot pizza. She closed her eyes and relished the mix of spice, tomatoes and cheese on her tongue, moaning just a little at its deliciousness. Had she been watching, she would have seen his broad smile as she inhaled the first piece.

"Take another drink. I promise you may have as much pizza as you wish," Rafael reassured her. His hand once again lowered to her knee.

The tingles that shimmered from his touch made her open her eyes to look at him questioningly. When he nodded again, she reached in and scooped up another steaming hot piece. Her head tilted a bit to the side as she turned to look at him once again. Impulsively, she held out the slice she had selected. "This one has lots of cheese. Would you like it?"

His smile could have illuminated the rest of the dark room.

She basked in his approval as she held the pizza a little closer to him. To her delight, he accepted her offering using his free hand. As she watched, he lifted the aromatic treat to his lips and took a bite. His "mmmm" of appreciation as he chewed made her wiggle in happiness on the soft mattress they shared.

"Eat, my sweet," he reminded her when she sat empty-handed, focused only on him. His thumb on her knee brushed softly over her skin. Nodding, she reached for another slice and took another hungry bite. As they sat and shared the delicious Italian pie, Mia felt like the entire world had disappeared around them.

The spotlight over her small space was intimate and exclusive of everything else. She had all his attention. There were no texts or business tasks to do. Rafael was hers. The surrounding darkness, which had felt threatening and isolating, now seemed to protect their privacy in a positive way.

He had chosen to make her the center of his attention. Mia did not have to opt to focus on him. She smiled to herself as she remembered all their exchanges over the internet. From the moment she had met him online, the mesmerizing man had dominated her thoughts. Rushing home each evening to check for messages, her life had become more… alive.

Finally, her stomach could hold no more. The last few remaining pizza slices were growing cold. Now, mingled together on one side was a pile of crusts. She'd been delighted to discover that the handsome man did not like to eat the crust either. Mia had partially sated her fierce hunger by inhaling that first piece in its entirety. Reaching the crust of the second, she rejected eating that crust to eat the yummy filled section of a third pizza slice. She'd hesitated to throw the hardened bread back into the box like she did at home until she'd seen him casually drop his into the box. Seeing them now all together made her feel strangely linked to Rafael.

Mia yawned behind a covering hand. She took a last sip of the carbonated treat and leaned forward to set it on the floor. Freezing in place as Rafael's fingers traced the faint marks that the flogger had left on her rounded buttocks, Mia smiled into the darkness at his appreciative touch. The pain of the strikes blended with the pleasure that he had brought her afterward.

As she sat back to look at him, Rafael looked so serious. Without thinking, her fingers reached forward to trace the lines between his brows and around his tense mouth. "What's wrong?" she whispered.

"Lie down, my sweet. You need to rest," the handsome man responded without answering her question. He helped her stretch out with her head cushioned on his muscled thigh. As his fingers brushed lightly over her tangled hair, Mia's eyes closed, the half-smile on her face easing the lines on his as Rafael watched over her. Stroked, touched, guarded, Mia relaxed into a deep sleep.

IT IS TIME, he thought as he forced himself away from Mia. Allowing her to leave the darkness was a risk, but he could not hold her captive here forever. To enjoy the relationship he desired, Rafael knew that she would need to submit voluntarily. He had set her on the correct path now. Whether she would choose to continue was up to Mia.

Entering his office, he turned on the large screen. Rafael strode to the wet bar and poured a generous amount of the aged, single malt scotch he preferred into a heavy tumbler. Cradling it between his hands to warm the mixture inside, Rafael inhaled the aroma.

When the memory of the scent of her heated desire fought for his attention, Rafael focused his gaze on her once again. His cock stiffened against the fine wool of his trousers. He shifted the glass to one hand and lifted it to take a healthy swig of the amber liquid as he adjusted his shaft. He would not allow himself to come without her now.

He'd already learned that Mia slept hard. Even when most upset, she slept longer than his usual six hours a night. Her health was tantamount now. Rafael would ensure that she was well tended in his care. Possessions needed to be carefully maintained—especially one that had taken so long to find.

Rafael settled in a chair to enjoy his whiskey. It was an extraordinary bottle. He'd only been able to find one, and considering the reach of his resources, that alone designated it as rare and precious. Unique belongings brought him pleasure. He did not take them for granted.

Her quiet breaths captivated him as he savored the rare liquor. A sudden laugh shattered the silence that filled his study. She would last much longer than that treasured bottle. Who knew, perhaps he'd make her his wife.

17

C uddling into the blanket that Rafael had draped over her body before leaving with the pizza box and the empty cans, Mia's eyes blinked open. *What?* She pushed herself up to sit and stared around. The lights were on. A few scattered shadows remained in the corners of the room and patterned on the floor near the bars.

The space should have seemed ordinary, completely bare of anything other than the few pieces of furniture that Mia had seen. A table over there where they'd had breakfast, the spanking bench with different implements hanging nearby. The toilet and her mat were the only other items in the vast area.

The mundane area didn't reassure her. Instead, Mia looked, around almost sad to see the mysteries unveiled. She pushed herself up to stand next to the mattress, wrapping the blanket around her shoulders. *What should she do?*

In the bars in front of her, a door had been opened. Hesitating near the safety that her mat had always offered, she wondered what to do. Mia took two baby steps toward the open door and froze as the speaker began.

"My sweet. Come to me," he gently ordered. His voice was even, not revealing any sign of anger.

Taking larger steps, Mia walked with growing confidence to the doorway.

Once outside the caged-in area, she spied a stairway to the right. Cautiously, ascending the stone stairs, she reached a large carved wooden door. She hesitated before placing her hand on the knob and pushing the door open. Climbing the last step, she emerged into a very sunny room filled with plants and flowers. Her hand shaded her eyes from the brightness as she felt the warmth of the sun on her face.

"Rafael? Are you here?" she asked.

"Close the door behind you, my sweet. If you are good, I will allow you to visit the darkness again," his voice came from behind her.

Whirling, Mia almost tripped over the blanket. Her first thought was to rush into his arms. As she took a step forward, his palm rose to stop her. She nodded and eagerly turned to follow his directions. Grasping the large doorknob, Mia struggled to push the heavy door closed. She could tell instantly the weathered wood was old and skilled hands had carved it years ago.

Once closed, her blue eyes rose to read the words carved into the wooden panels.

May you escape
to the freedom that
darkness offers.

Her hand rose to trace the second to last word. Darkness. With a gasp, she looked back at Rafael. She had been trapped in the darkness for however long. The frightening environment had become a haven for her. There, she had experienced a stronger connection with Rafael than with any of the men she had dated in the past.

Snatching that hand back to her chest, Mia slowly turned to look at him. "Is it over?" Her voice trembled despite her attempt to keep it steady.

His hand reached out to her. "Come here, my sweet."

Mia flew to his side and threw her arms around his waist. She didn't want to leave him. He'd fascinated her online, and with each conversation, she'd lost a bit of her heart. Being taken and trapped in the basement could have been traumatic, but it was like the wish on the door. There had been freedom in the darkness. He had sheltered her from the surrounding world, forcing her to experience some of her fantasies.

"Don't send me away," she whispered as she attempted to memorize everything about him. His hair! Now, she knew it was the deepest shade of brown.

"You belong to me. I knew that after just a few short conversations with you. You just need to realize it. Come. Let me take care of you," he commanded. Stepping away from her, Rafael took her hand and led her through the sunroom.

Glancing into the beautiful rooms as he escorted her through the house and up a large curved staircase, Mia smiled at the elegant home that must match his refined public self. She felt even closer to him. Rafael had shown her the hidden side of himself. One that she bet very few people had ever seen.

As they walked into a large bathroom, Mia pushed her musings out of her mind to watch the charismatic man. Rafael leaned over to start the water gushing into an immense clawfoot tub that sat at the end of the beautiful room. He released her hand to open one of the crystal jars of bath salts and poured a generous portion into the warm water. Instantly, the scent of lavender spread throughout the room.

Mia glimpsed herself in the mirror. Horrified by the sight of her rumpled hair and lack of makeup, she walked forward to inspect herself. Her battered hands rose to comb through the birds' nest her hair had become. When his handsome, well-groomed face appeared behind her, Mia dropped her head down so that Rafael wouldn't be able to see her face.

One strong hand reached out to pick up a silver-backed hairbrush. The young woman peeked up at the mirror as Rafael began to tame her snarls gently. Now, in the bright lighting of the bathroom, Mia's blue eyes devoured his features and expression as he worked carefully to avoid hurting her.

They'd exchanged photos after they had been talking for a month.

Rafael's picture had obviously been taken on a business trip to a large city. Standing in the shade of a towering office building, he drew attention. Dressed immaculately in a gray suit, Rafael had exuded power and importance effortlessly. Mia had stared at this picture frequently, searching for clues about where and who he was. She'd hated not knowing what color his eyes were under the dark sunglasses. Now, she knew.

Rafael was elegant, professionally dressed as always. She could now see that those captivating eyes were dark brown bordering on black. Set in a rectangular face with a chiseled jawline, his gaze could pin her in place or make her warm in places like she had never experienced before.

As he stood in front of the vanity, the bright lighting glinted off the silver in his hair. That small bit of gray just seemed to make him more attractive in a worldly, experienced way. She softly smiled at that thought.

"What are you thinking?" he asked, curious about her expression.

"We are so different," she said honestly. "I wish I knew all that you know."

"I LIKE your mind just as it is." He smiled at her in the mirror. His eyes contemplated the young woman before him who he had researched so thoroughly. Rafael knew that she was twenty-seven. His investigations of her background had revealed three boyfriends—only one had been serious. Two at the university and one from the office building where she worked now.

His Mia was a beautiful woman. Especially now, he thought. Her face was clear of any makeup or artifice, showcasing her wide blue eyes and shoulder-length brown hair. He felt that he was seeing the real Mia—not the one she usually showed the rest of the world.

Rafael finished brushing the worst of the tangles from her straight hair, "In fact, I like all of you, just as you are. Mine." He set the heavy, silver brush down on the granite vanity with a definitive click before carefully taking off his expensive watch and setting it down as well.

Watching her shiver, Rafael enjoyed her body's response to his solemn words. There was no doubt that she recognized he had claimed her. When his strong hands tugged the blanket from her hands, her fingers clenched automatically on the soft fabric. As she watched in the mirror, his gentle smile disappeared. Those beautiful lips hardened, warning her before his hand pulled harder, removing the blanket from her grip.

"Mine to dress or mine to undress. It is important to remember that a possession belongs to the owner, to cherish or to correct." His fingers wandered over a few faint flogging marks that remained. When those dark eyes met her shocked blue gaze, he added, "Come now, my sweet. It is time for your bath." Taking her hand, he led her to the large soaking tub. Rafael wrapped his hands around her waist to steady Mia as she stepped into the tub.

THE WARM STEAMY water was fragrant and silky around her as she sank into the tub with a sigh of enjoyment. Mia leaned against the sloped back of the tub and closed her eyes to savor the luxury of this bath. A whisper of movement came from behind her. Starting to open her eyes and tilt her head back to look, Mia panicked as Rafael's powerful hands wrapped around her shoulders and pressed down.

Without time to protest, Mia's head slid under the surface of the water. Panicking, she struggled to sit up, fighting the hands that held her under the surface. The ceramic coating on the inside of the tub did not allow her to gain any traction, especially with the addition of the silky bath salts.

Mia's eyes burned as she stared up through the murky water at the handsome man who loomed over her. His face was composed as he watched her struggle under the water. *He's going to kill me!* The terror-stricken thought raced through her head seconds before he pulled her up from the water.

Gasping for air, Mia clung to the sides of the tub. She tried to scramble from the water, but he held her in place. Trying to get away from his touch, Mia's movements were easily controlled by the seemingly unaffected man. Terrified, she froze in the tub. Her eyes burned from the additives mingled throughout the water. She tried to clear her vision by rubbing her eyes, but her wet hands only spread more of the bath salts.

"Do not move," he instructed.

Immediately, she nodded. Her mind raced as she realized that holding her under the water had been retribution for resisting Rafael's pull on the blanket. Remaining perfectly still, she watched him walk to the counter and open a drawer. When he returned with a wet washcloth and a new packet of eye drops, Mia held perfectly still as he wiped her eyes carefully with the damp cloth before dropping several eye drops into each blue eye to wash away the chemicals that burned.

"It would be wise to keep your eyes closed next time," he suggested without emotion as he knelt by the side of the tub.

"You're going to try to kill me again?" she choked out.

"You belong to me, Mia. It is up to me to teach you how to behave correctly. There was no risk that you would die." His tone was eerily calm. "Now, your hair is wet. I think you will need to have it cleaned."

Mia sat perfectly still in the tub as he applied sweet-smelling shampoo on her sodden brown hair. His fingers mixed the cleanser into the brown locks and scrubbed gently at her scalp. Her eyes closed at the pampering treatment before flashing back open. She didn't want him to surprise her again.

When her hair was squeaky clean, he rinsed out the shampoo with a sprayer attached to the faucet. The feel of the water pouring over her hair brought back the panic she had felt as the warm liquid had covered her head. Instantly, she began to scramble wildly from the tub.

Rafael gathered her against his muscular body. His hand brushed her still soapy hair from her face before beginning to brush down her back to comfort her. "My sweet, have you done anything wrong?" he asked in a soft tone.

"Noooo!" she wailed against him.

"Then you have nothing to fear," he reassured her. Holding her tightly against his body until her beating heart calmed, the handsome man did not rush her or become impatient. He simply held her in his arms.

Finally, Mia pushed slightly away from his body. His drenched shirt was plastered against his chest. Scared that she had messed up again, Mia rushed to apologize, "Sorry. I shouldn't have gotten you wet." Her fingers plucked the almost transparent fabric away from his firm chest.

"You do not need to apologize, my sweet. You are still learning." Rafael leaned back slightly and unbuttoned his shirt.

Her eyes focused on the deft movements of his fingers. As each button slid free, he revealed more of his chest. Mia had never seen him even casually dressed. His crisp, white dress shirts were always immaculate. Finally, Rafael pulled the tail of the shirt from his waistline to unbutton the last two closures. As he shrugged out of the wet garment, her blue eyes devoured the masculine grace he revealed.

Toned and fit, Rafael's body revealed the discipline with which he lived his life. Without an inch of spare flesh, his form was almost perfection. Deep brown hair scattered over his chest in just the right amount to invite fingers to curl within them and perhaps tug a bit. Her eyes jumped to the ragged scar running just below his collarbone.

"What happened?" she blurted out as her fingers reached out without thought to touch the healed injury.

"Come, my sweet. Close your eyes. Allow me to rinse your hair. The water will cool soon," Rafael urged, ignoring her question as he lifted the sprayer and tilted back her head to rinse the last of the suds from her hair.

Mia understood. She would only know those things he chose to tell her. She closed her eyes and allowed him to take care of her hair. When he'd stroked a leave-in conditioner through her hair and wrapped a towel like a turban around her head, Rafael's attention turned to Mia's body.

"Close your eyes, my sweet," he directed as he dipped a washcloth into the water.

She hesitated slightly and saw his face harden. Slamming her eyes shut, Mia held her breath.

"Thank you, my sweet."

Within seconds, she felt the soft fabric touch her face. He spread the suds across her face and throat, avoiding getting soap into her eyes. After quickly wiping the lather away, he began bathing her arms. Mia's eyes flashed back open to watch him carefully clean any dirt from her stay in the basement from her skin.

She inhaled sharply as the cloth rubbed over her small breasts. Arousal shimmered inside her body as his thumbs brushed over those beaded tips. Her eyes darted to his face, and inside she grew warmer upon seeing the desire written on his handsome face. Mia tried to hold on to the terror that she had felt earlier—to remember just what this man was capable of doing. Her mind instead chose to thrill at his touch on her body. Smoothing over her legs with the cloth, Rafael washed every toe as she anticipated feeling his hand on more intimate areas.

"Spread your legs, my sweet," he commanded.

She'd learned her lesson. Immediately, she bent her legs and allowed her knees to fall to the sides. Watching with equal amounts of anticipation and apprehension, Mia kept her eyes glued to that cloth as it glided down one inner thigh before stopping.

"What?" burst from her lips before she could stop it. Quickly, she raised her eyes to meet his. Relaxing just a bit at the amusement dancing in his dark eyes, she quickly put her hand over her mouth to stop her outbursts.

"Hand down, my sweet. I always want to hear your questions and your sounds of enjoyment. Lie back against the tub and relax. Let me take care of you," he instructed.

Waging a battle in her mind over each inch, Mia leaned back slowly. Only when her shoulders pressed against the porcelain did Rafael move the cloth through the water to glide over the sparse hair at the junction of her thighs. Without a pause or tiny hesitation, his hand drew the washcloth through the pink folds usually hidden between her legs.

His other hand reached under her lower back to lift her hips slightly. Mia started to buck up into a seated position but remained reclined when those piercing eyes rose to look at her in a warning. She immediately pressed her shoulders back against the tub's edge.

Satisfied, his gaze returned to the washcloth. Rafael pressed the cloth past the clenched, small opening between her buttocks to finish her bath before releasing the washcloth to drift slowly to the bottom of the tub. One hand still held her bottom slightly elevated off the tub surface. The other hand rose to lie against one creamy thigh as his thumb brushed through her pink folds. Lightly back and forth, that teasing digit glided over her swelling clitoris

That lifting hand under her hips robbed her of any movement, rendering her off-balance in the slippery tub. Not that she would have resisted his attentions. She knew the pleasure that he could give her. Since the water had begun gushing into the tub, Mia had fought her growing arousal. The scare of being held underwater should have erased her desire. But it didn't.

18

Later, as she stared into the bathroom mirror, the heat of his body behind her warmed Mia's body. It still tingled with the aftereffects of Rafael's skilled caresses. He had brought her to orgasm twice before lifting her from the water.

After drying her swaying body, Rafael unwrapped her hair and quickly combed it into place. His patience and unwillingness to hurt her as he detangled her hair clashed with his actions earlier to punish her.

Learning quickly to do what he asked without hesitation or question, Mia enjoyed his care. Her sated eyes stared at him in the mirror as he tended her hair. She memorized his fit body and stared hungrily at the thick erection that pressed against his fly.

Why didn't he have sex with her? He hadn't even kissed her. Somehow, she knew not to ask. They were on his time schedule. Not hers.

When he had smoothed her skin with luxurious body cream, Rafael interrupted her thoughts to ask, "Do you need to use the restroom?"

At her embarrassed nod, he opened a door to reveal the enclosed toilet. Waiting outside for her, Rafael did not appear impatient but merely lounged against the opposing wall. Mia appreciated the small bit of privacy. Quickly using the toilet, she emerged and washed her hands before returning to his side.

Rafael wrapped an arm around her waist and led her into the attached bedroom. Mia looked around in amazement at the beautifully decorated room and the enormous bed that dominated the space as he walked into the attached master closet to retrieve a dry shirt.

"This is lovely," she complimented as he emerged from what looked like a massive space.

"Thank you," he answered without elaborating. "Come, my sweet. I need to get some work done. You can rest while I review some files."

"Do you have a spare computer or phone? I would love to let everyone know that I am safe," she dared to suggest.

"You are on vacation as far as everyone knows. No one has worried about you. They know that you are having a good time," Rafael answered absentmindedly as his eyes scanned her nude body.

Saying nothing else, he turned and reentered the closet only to return a few seconds later with a soft flannel shirt. Rafael unfastened all the buttons before helping her into the garment. "I do not wish you to become ill. While I prefer to see your body, I want to protect you from a chill more."

She tried to stand completely still, but his fingers slid gently against her skin as he fit each button carefully into the correct buttonhole. His touch made her shiver as she remembered the caresses he'd lavished on her body. "Do I ever get to touch you?" she dared to ask. "May I kiss you?"

He smiled at her as he finished the last button. "We will kiss when you have proven your loyalty to me. Touching, we will enjoy long before our lips meet. A kiss is special."

Bewildered by his response, Mia followed him silently when he took her hand. Padding barefoot through the large house, the young woman caught glimpses of staff members working. Rafael continued through the house until he came to a closed doorway. Pulling keys from his pocket, the man, once again wearing a crisp dress shirt, unlocked the door and pulled her inside. Once inside, he locked the door to seal them inside.

Mia looked around the large office space, trying to figure out what specifically this obviously successful businessman did. A massive bank of screens dominated one wall. Without giving her time to take everything in, Rafael tugged her over to an oversized wooden desk. As they moved behind it, Mia noticed a large cushiony mat to the right of the office chair on the floor.

"Take a seat, Mia. You will need to entertain yourself. There is a variety of office supplies in the bottom drawer. Help yourself to the paper, pens, markers. Do not get off your mat without permission. Do not interrupt me with something frivolous," he warned, meeting her eyes to make sure she understood.

When she nodded hesitantly, he pointed to the mat before sitting down in the large office chair and powering on his computer. Mia sunk to the mat on the floor and lay quietly on her side. Her mouth pursed and twisted to the side as she tried to decide how she felt about sitting on the floor at his feet. She didn't think she liked it too much.

Opening her mouth to say something snarky, Mia heard him speak in fluent Mandarin Chinese. When a lyrical voice spoke back in the same Eastern language, Mia snapped her mouth closed and listened intently. She'd had a teacher in elementary school who knew a bit of Mandarin and had delighted in sharing small bits of the language with the students in Mia's class.

Recognizing the sounds and rhythm of the language, she struggled to follow his conversation. Unsuccessful at doing anything more than picking out a very few familiar words, Mia tried to recall the small amount of information he had shared with her during their online conversations. Rafael had easily focused each interaction on her, and she had basked in his attention without asking a flurry of questions.

When that conversation ended, Mia started to comment on his language ability. "I didn't know you spoke…"

Her words cut out as Rafael's hand lifted and drifted casually below the surface of the desk as he began another conversation. When his fingers curved around her shoulder to tighten warningly, Mia closed her mouth with a snap.

Sitting there hidden from the view of whoever Rafael spoke with,

Mia's anger multiplied. The more she thought about being a hidden embarrassment, the more steam built up inside her. Finally, she exploded. Pulling open the bottom drawer that he'd filled with busywork for her, Mia slammed it shut, making as much noise as possible.

Without pausing in his conversation, Rafael grabbed the back of her still-damp hair and lifted his hand up. The pain brought tears to her eyes as she stood to attempt to get close enough to his hand to ease the pull on her scalp. The conversation continued between him and the businessman on the screen. Rafael trapped her between the desk and his chair and began unbuttoning the soft, warm shirt wrapped around her nude body.

Mia looked with panic over her shoulder at the man who was watching. She hissed, "Rafael. Rafael. Stop. I'm sorry. I lost my temper."

The businessman's hands never hesitated. Soon, he pushed the garment over her shoulders. Mia tried to stop him or free herself, but Rafael was too strong. He overpowered her with ease. Before he pushed his chair back, Rafael hooked one polished leather dress shoe around one of Mia's ankles. The momentum of the rollers on the carpet off-balanced the young woman, and she found herself stretched out over his lap with her bottom pointed to the ceiling.

Rafael captured both of her hands behind her back, trapping her across his thighs. Her toes barely touched the floor. Even more concerning to Mia, when she reared up and turned her head to look back at the screen, she made eye contact with the other businessman. He could see everything that was happening. Mia dropped back into place, trying to hide as much of her body from the other man's view.

With his free hand, Rafael opened the second to the bottom drawer. Pulling out two wide items, he placed them on the desk in front of him. To her horror, Rafael changed the conversation.

Speaking in English, he indicated the paddles on the table, "My apologies, comrade. My possession is new and untrained. I am sorry to interrupt our conversation, but I feel that poor behavior should be addressed immediately. If you don't mind?"

"I would suggest the red one. It appears to be the sturdiest," the Russian answered with a heavy accent.

"No, Rafael. I'm sorry…" Mia pleaded before yelping as the red paddle smacked against her bottom. To her astonishment, the conversation resumed between the two men. She knew that the Russian was watching. Mia could feel his eyes on her bare flesh. Refusing to look at him to see condemnation in the stranger's eyes, Mia kept her face pressed against Rafael's calf.

Over and over, Rafael applied the sturdy instrument to her bottom and upper thighs. The flesh turned pink immediately and then red blossomed shockingly on the pale skin. He continued to spank her until Mia stopped squirming on his lap and hung limply. At her total submission, Rafael replaced the two paddles inside the desk and closed the drawer.

The conversation between the two businessmen continued as if nothing out of the norm had just taken place. Rafael reached past her to snare his tablet. He placed this on the small of Mia's back before beginning to rub her spanked bottom. He typed a few words and then replaced the tablet on his desk.

To Mia's surprise, he released her arms and lifted her to lie against his chest. Her gasp of pain as her weight settled on her punished bottom brought faint smiles to each man's lips. His warm hands smoothed over her body again and again as Rafael rocked the chair underneath them.

Clinging to his crisp dress shirt as her tears wet the fabric below her cheek, Mia missed their reaction to her small distressed sound as she berated herself for disappointing him. She knew that she shouldn't make a noise. *Why did I push him?* she asked herself, even though she already knew the answer. She had wanted to test him. Would he be trapped into ignoring her flagrant misbehavior due to his business call or not? She realized now that he would deal with her swiftly despite the audience.

Within a few minutes, she heard him thank the businessman on the other side of the world for his time and disconnect the phone call. Mia expected to hear the Russian say something derogatory about her, but there was no mention of her or her spanking. With wonder, she realized that in Rafael's world, his colleagues had accepted her appearance and punishment without question. The other man had even suggested which paddle to use as if this were a normal conversation. She didn't understand this unknown world that she'd become a part of, but she was learning the rules were much different.

Rafael's office door clicked as the lock was disengaged. Mia looked up in shock as the door swung open. A suited gentleman walked across the office carpeting to place a silver tray bearing two bottles of water on the desk in front of the businessman before hanging a new starched shirt on the handle of a nearby cabinet. Mia curled against the solid, warm body below her, trying to hide her nudity. With her eyes hidden, she didn't notice that the butler never looked directly at her but turned and left the office at his boss' nod of thanks.

"Here, my sweet. Drink some water. You will need to learn to behave differently now that you are with me," Rafael directed as he opened the water and held the cold bottle to her lips. He observed her carefully as she drank several sips before allowing her to take the bottle in her own shaking hands.

"That man saw me," she whispered.

"He would not have known for sure you were there had you sat quietly as I clearly instructed," Rafael mentioned nonchalantly as he opened a desk drawer to remove a box of tissues. Pulling several out, he wiped her eyes and nose.

"You hurt me," she accused.

"I did," he answered without remorse. Reaching past Mia to the desk, Rafael casually moved all the papers stretched before him and his tablet to the side. Taking the water bottle from her, he lifted her effortlessly to sit on the desk before him. "Lie back on my desk, my sweet," Rafael sternly commanded.

Bewildered, Mia followed his directions and lowered herself to her forearms. She watched him roll his chair away from her before tugging her mat into the space between them. Moving her thighs wide apart, Rafael knelt on the mattress and pulled her reddened bottom to the edge of his desk. She gasped as Rafael lowered his mouth to taste her.

"Mmmm," he murmured as if savoring the flavor of her intimate juices. Raising his head slightly to meet her eyes, Rafael noted, "You are soaked, my sweet. I will continue to pleasure you until you come twice." He looked at his watch and added, "You have five minutes before my next phone call, or you will again have an audience for our private moments."

"What?" she cried as his mouth lowered to nibble at her pink folds. Rafael did not pause to answer her.

RAFAEL HAD BEEN FASTENING the last two buttons on his fresh shirt when the phone call had activated on the screen before him. Mia curled nude on the carpet at his feet. Rafael had locked the mat in the cabinet behind them. She would need to earn the privilege back. This time Mia was quiet as she squeezed her inner thighs together frequently to enjoy the lasting tingles that remained from her orgasms. Moving slightly to pillow her head on his smooth leather shoes, she drifted off to sleep with a faint smile on her lips, totally missing the matching curve of his.

WHILE SHE SLEPT, Rafael completed his urgent meetings for the day. The rest his assistant could handle. Pulling up her social media accounts, Rafael checked to see if anyone had contacted her. Just as he had anticipated, Mia's relationships and friendships were distant. No one had become concerned when she had been out of contact for days.

With that task completed, Rafael contemplated the small form stretched on the carpet. Although he'd never admit it, he enjoyed her fire, and each burst of rebellion revealed a bit more of her personality. She craved his dominance, but she would never be meek and mild.

He selected a number on his phone he called extremely rarely. It was answered after only one ring. "Miguel, I hope I am not interrupting anything?" he asked to be congenial. Rafael didn't care if his call arrived at the worst moment. At his brother's answer, he knew Miguel realized that as well.

"The house is burning down around me, but I can stop my flight to chat for a few seconds before the roof collapses upon me." His brother's dry humor made him laugh aloud. "Pray tell. What has moved you to contact me?"

"I've found her."

The background noise that surrounded Miguel drew softer, as if he were moving to a more secluded location. After a minute, the other man commented, "Congratulations, brother. I had hoped that I would find my match first."

"You always were the competitive one," Rafael commented lightly.

An explosion of laughter burst through the phone lines. "Right. You beat me into this world by two minutes, and I've been running to try to catch up ever since. I'd heard that you'd leased our mama's old apartment," Miguel mentioned casually.

"Yes."

When Rafael didn't add to his comment, his brother continued, "Perhaps I need to borrow that apartment, dear brother. That must have been the lucky charm." After a slight pause, he added, "Our parents would be pleased for you, Rafael. I also am glad to hear your news."

"Thank you, Miguel. I hope you find your one." He also paused to reflect on his words. "If the apartment can assist you as well, it will be vacant soon."

"Thank you, brother."

When they disconnected, Rafael sat quietly contemplating the young woman at his feet. It was rare that he stopped working to appreciate the view and engage in small talk with his brother. Mia had changed his life already as well. They would be good for each other, he decided, before leaning back in his chair to make plans for their future.

19

At dinner that night, Mia was surprised to be seated at the table with Rafael. The large dining room could have easily hosted forty guests for a meal. The young woman hunched her shoulders to hide her body as the servants bustled around the two of them at the large table in the elegant, formal dining room.

"Shoulders back, my sweet," Rafael ordered as he shook out his linen napkin to lay it across his lap.

Forcing herself to follow his commands, Mia cursed her impetuous actions that had resulted in the removal of the shirt he had allowed her to wear as well as the still-painful bottom that she sat on. As she sat back against the chair, the aloof butler had placed her own napkin over her lap before motioning the servers to ladle a delicious-smelling soup into the bowls before them. Overwhelmed by dishes and silverware in front of her, Mia hoped that she wouldn't make a fool of herself.

"Ahem." Rafael cleared his throat before lifting the outermost spoon to dip it into his soup.

Nodding in relief, Mia picked up her spoon and followed his lead. Her eyes traced the wide shoulders of the handsome man at the head of the table. Rafael had dressed for dinner as she watched. An elegant gown had hung in the doorway to the master bathroom as he changed.

She knew that had she not acted in anger, she would have been wearing the beautiful silver gown.

Shrugging away the past mistake, Mia promised herself that she would please him in the future. She raised the spoon and tasted the soup carefully. Deliciousness exploded over her taste buds, making her aware of how hungry she was. Immediately, she raised another spoonful to her mouth.

"I have an excellent chef, my sweet. He will be glad to see that you enjoy his food." Rafael smiled at her, enjoying her obvious appreciation of the soup before him. When she hesitated self-consciously, he encouraged her, "Eat, Mia. You are hungry."

Relieved, Mia ate several more spoonfuls of soup before pausing to ask, "Do you always eat dinner here in this beautiful room?"

"Yes, my sweet. Why have a dining room if you do not use it? I will admit that it is much more pleasurable to have your company than to dine alone. I will host some dinner parties now that you are here," he remarked casually.

Before she could reconsider her words, Mia blurted, "Will I be able to wear clothes?" Her hand covered her mouth as the last syllable left her lips. She stared at him, hoping that her question would not have angered him. To her relief, he laughed.

"That will be up to you, my sweet," he answered. Changing the subject, he told her, "Tomorrow, a hair stylist and groomer will come to attend to you."

Her free hand lifted to her hair to run through the brown strands. Mia wanted to ask what the stylist would do to her, but she was learning that it was best not to question Rafael. That second word popped into her mind. Didn't they call people who cut dogs' hair groomers? What was that person going to do to her?

She forced her hand back down to her lap as she ate another spoonful of the delicious soup. Deliberately, she shifted on her sore buttocks to remind herself of the punishment she could risk. Silence fell over the table as they both ate. When she finished her soup, the bowl was whisked away by a silent server.

Mia glanced up to see him watching her with a slight smile of approval. Without thinking, her lips spread in a wide grin. She had pleased him. It was a thrilling feeling. Her lips twisted slightly together as she struggled to find a way to continue to make him happy.

"Mia, you may ask me questions if you wish," he informed her softly.

"Are you married?" she blurted, surprising herself.

"No, my sweet. I have not married yet. I have been searching for the right woman to make mine," he answered without hesitation.

They were silent as the next course was placed in front of them. It was a small filet of steak and beautifully arranged vegetables. They both ate for a few minutes, enjoying the main course. Mia was not used to eating so well. For her, this was quite a treat—like eating in a restaurant for her birthday.

"When's your birthday?" she curiously asked.

Rafael laughed with delight at the seemingly random question. "My birthday is on April 14. Next year, I will be forty-seven years old. Does that seem ancient to you?" he asked with a smile.

"I'm twenty-seven," she answered before realizing that he already knew that. "You know so much about me, and I know virtually nothing about you."

"I am exactly what you see—a businessman who has created a successful life for myself through long hours, hard work, and never-ending control."

"Sounds lonely," she remarked without thinking as she took another bite of the delicious steak. When he didn't answer, she looked up, afraid that she had been too honest. She caught him contemplating her seriously. She smiled, hopeful that she wasn't in trouble, and relaxed a bit when he smiled back.

"At times, very lonely, my sweet."

———

FOR ONCE, Rafael didn't resent the time that a meal kept him from his business. He watched the lovely young woman closely as she ate her meal. Even when obviously famished, Mia had exhibited lovely table manners. Quickly, he understood that her background did not include fine dining and the concept of multiple courses. Her consternation at the array of forks had been enchanting.

As the meal continued, Mia's appetite waned as she sated her hunger. Rafael was sure that she would have licked the soup bowl clean if she had been alone. Only the delicious chocolate tart for dessert had revitalized her desire for food.

She was a beautiful addition to his table. While he usually ate at his desk, the chef had prepared this lovely feast upon hearing that Mia would dine with Rafael. His well-trained staff did not react to her lovely form displayed completely at the table. He had no doubt that Mia would learn from this experience and improve her behavior.

She would need frequent reminders of her role as she adjusted. This would not be the last time she dined nude with a red bottom. At least this time, she had been able to sit. When a thought pinged into his mind, Rafael pulled out his phone to leave himself a reminder: *Order a stripping pad for a floor stripper. Check to see if the dimensions are comparable to a chair.*

"What's that for?" she blurted, before looking like she'd really preferred to have not asked.

"For your chair. A naughty bottom shouldn't have something soft to sit on, right?" To his delight, she nodded automatically before freezing as she realized that she was the one destined to be sitting on an abrasive pad.

He redirected her thoughts. "Finish your tart. It's almost time for bed." When she wiggled in delight, another thought popped into his mind. "Please ask the chef to join us," he requested of one of the waitstaff.

Rapidly, his white-jacketed chef appeared at his elbow. "Sir, I hope the meal was pleasing?"

"It was delicious. Mia quite enjoyed the soup and the chocolate tart. I enjoyed everything. I believe there was a new marinade for the steak?" he asked, making pleasant conversation. He'd stolen his chef from a downtown restaurant when he'd been delighted with his meal. Paying him an extravagant salary with a large food budget and much-improved working hours had convinced him that working in the private sector was acceptable.

"You are very discerning, Mr. Montalvo. It was a whiskey peppercorn concoction I have been playing with," the chef admitted with a wide smile. His shoulders relaxed down from his ears.

"Delicious!" Rafael declared before leaning forward confidentially. "I would like you to add something to your market list. Please begin stocking a supply of fresh ginger. Ask the supplier for several thick fingers of the root that would be appropriate to be peeled and used for figging."

"Figging, sir?" The chef's eyes roamed to the nude young woman at the table.

"Yes. You've understood me completely. Make sure you have this on hand from now on," he said, nodding to dismiss the chef from the table.

"What's figging?" Mia whispered.

"You don't want to find out."

20

With a tummy pooching slightly from the delicious meal, Mia accepted quickly when Rafael suggested walking in the garden. She needed to escape that final conversation. Very conscious of her nudity, the young woman walked slightly behind the businessman as they passed through the house. Rafael's well-trained staff did not make eye contact with her or stare.

She didn't understand. Were they used to having naked women walking around here? Wrinkling her nose in anger at that thought, Mia did not notice that Rafael had stopped to open the garden doors. With a body-jarring impact, she slammed into the back of him.

"Uff! My sweet, are you okay?" Rafael turned to run his hands down her arms.

"Sorry. I should have been watching where I was going," she muttered, avoiding his eyes.

"What is wrong, my sweet? Think carefully before you answer. I do not wish to be lied to," Rafael warned. When she hesitated, he took her hand and pulled her through the doorway and out into the fragrant garden. Moving down a concrete pathway to reach a bench, he sat down and pulled her onto his lap. When she started to scramble off,

Rafael pinched her blistered bottom to remind her to behave. She froze in place.

"What is wrong?" he repeated.

"The people who work here... are they used to seeing your women wandering naked around your house?" The words tumbled from her lips. She couldn't look at him. Mia stared at her hands twisting together on her lap. When he didn't answer immediately, she forced herself to try to relax. Leaning into the crook of his neck, she inhaled. Sandalwood. Unable to resist, Mia pressed her lips to the crisp collar that encircled his neck.

"Ah, my sweet. How you please me." Rafael wrapped his arms around her to squeeze her tight to his hard body. "My staff are well trained in all ways. They are, however, not used to seeing naked, young women wandering around my house."

"Or staying in the basement?" she dared to ask.

"No," he said with a chuckle.

"Are you ever going to kiss me? Or make love to me?" While he was answering her questions, she figured she might as well go for broke.

"Yes."

"Yes?" she asked, leaning back to look at him.

"Yes. Stand up, my sweet," Rafael ordered, lifting her onto her feet.

She whirled to look at him closely. Was he going to kiss her now? She watched as he stood and walked back into the house. Was he leaving her? Mia stood frozen in place, arguing internally whether she should follow or stay by the bench.

At the door, Rafael turned and looked surprised to see her a distance away. He held his hand out to her. "My sweet?"

Mia ran toward him, unmindful of the bouncing of her small breasts and the concrete under her bare feet. Reaching him, she took his extended hand and clung to it. "I didn't know what to do," she explained.

Rafael leaned in close. Mia held her breath, hoping he would kiss her, but his cheek simply brushed hers lightly as he whispered into her ear, "Stay with me always."

Grabbing hold of this slight hint of attachment, Mia nodded.

When he stepped back to smile at her fondly, the young woman's heart skipped a beat. She didn't understand how his approval had become so vital, but she wanted it—badly. The attractive older man had become the center of her world so quickly. This time when he opened the door and held it for her, Mia knew that she would follow him anywhere. *He wants me.*

She trailed behind him up the wide staircase and back to the master bedroom. There now, next to the bed, lay an identical mat to the one she had slept on in the darkness. The spotlight had revealed the pattern woven in the cover. Mia looked at Rafael in surprise. Was she not going to sleep with him?

"Come, my sweet. Let's get ready for bed," he invited as he drew her into the bathroom. Handing her an unwrapped toothbrush and toothpaste, Rafael laughed at her groan of excitement. "Brush your teeth and use the toilet. Stay here when you're finished," he directed as his fingers unbuttoned that crisp dress shirt.

Her eyes stayed glued on him as the shirt spread apart to reveal his broad chest and crisp black hair peppered with gray. Biting her lower lip as he tugged his shirt from his waistband, Mia met his smiling eyes.

"Brush your teeth, my sweet," he reminded her.

Mia looked down at the toothbrush still in its container. She forced her grip to relax, and she opened her hand. The grooves in her hand testified to her intense focus on Rafael as he undressed. She quickly pulled open the package and removed the toothbrush. Squeezing toothpaste over the bristles, she began brushing her teeth.

A flash of motion caught her eye, and she turned to see a bare-chested Rafael coiling his belt in a circle. He walked forward to set it on the vanity next to her. Moving the toothbrush automatically in her mouth, Mia's eyes traced down his muscular chest to watch his fingers unbutton his sleek trousers and draw the zipper down slowly. When his hands pushed the trousers over his hips, a thin line of toothpaste slid from the corner of her mouth.

Appalled, she turned to the sink and wiped away the drool. A vivid red blush blossomed over her cheeks, extending to the top of her chest.

Mia watched that hand pluck the belt from the vanity. Her eyes jumped to the mirror to watch him walk into the large master closet. When he disappeared from her view, Mia quickly finished brushing her teeth and rinsed her mouth.

As she turned to walk to the enclosed toilet, Rafael emerged from the closet. She stopped to stare at his nude body as he walked to the shower stall. His body was lean and fit. Not overmuscled or artificial, Rafael's body moved in perfect coordination as if he were a sleek jungle cat. As he walked toward her, his eyes captured her blue ones, pinning her in place as if she were prey.

"Use the toilet, my sweet. Then sit on the vanity and wait for me. Do not touch yourself," Rafael demanded before turning to walk into the large clear glass shower stall.

Mia moaned softly as the water began pouring down into the shower, drenching Rafael's incredible form. His hands smoothed thick soap over his body. When the scent of sandalwood met her nose, Mia's eyes closed in enjoyment. When they opened, her blue eyes met his dark eyes through the now steamy glass. Embarrassed to have been caught staring, Mia darted away to the toilet.

A short time later with damp, washed hands, Mia laid down a towel before hopping up onto the vanity. Rafael had leaned over to clean his toes, giving her a perfect view of his firm butt. She squeezed her legs together in response to the arousing show that she watched.

Rafael stood and turned to face the spray to rinse the soap from his body. The handsome man provided Mia with the chance to see his profile. The breath caught in her throat. His entire body was hard. Rafael's thick shaft thrust proudly upward, reaching toward his flat stomach.

Unaware of her actions, Mia licked her lips. She began to slide from the vanity but remembered his directions at the last second. Scooting back, her blue eyes never left his body as he turned off the shower and turned to face her through the fogged glass.

She didn't hurry. Mia forced her eyes to lift from his erection to slide over his abs and chest before reaching his dark eyes. Hunger poured from that dark gaze.

With a click, Rafael pushed open the door and stepped out. Reaching for a thick towel, he dried himself off in slow, unhurried movements. His eyes roamed down her body, pausing here and there.

Unable to stop herself, Mia's knees slid slightly apart on the vanity. Moving her hands behind her to rest on the cold surface, she thrust her shoulders back, putting herself on display for his enjoyment. She watched as he dropped the towel on the floor and stalked forward.

His hands seized her waist as she lifted her lips for the kiss she was sure was coming. Gasping, Mia reached out for stability as his hand turned her away from him to face the mirror. He quickly pressed her breasts down to the towel-covered vanity. With one hand, he held her pinned to the soft terry cloth as the other stroked down her back and over her reddened bottom. After pinching one small cheek to draw a gasp from her, Rafael roughly moved her feet wide apart with his damp calf as his fingers dived into the wetness that waited for him.

"Yes!" Mia moaned in encouragement as she looked at his passion-hardened expression in the mirror. "Please, Rafael. Make love to me!"

His dark eyes met hers. "Our joining will not be mundane lovemaking, my sweet," he growled in warning.

Swallowing hard, Mia knew she craved his touch. "I know," she whispered.

Immediately, his two fingers of his hand thrust into her tight channel. Her body clamped down on his invasion, trying to hold him inside her as she shivered with delight.

"Nooo!" she howled as his fingers glided out of her body.

There was no response to her protest as those fingers withdrew from her vagina. His fingertips lightly traced that swollen bud poised atop her entrance, making Mia's dazed blue eyes close with pleasure. She lifted onto her toes, trying to press back against him, but his large hand anchored her securely to the vanity. To her delight, his fingers pressed back inside her body, filling the ache he had awoken before withdrawing to leave her yearning for more.

Mia's eyes flashed open at the rattle of a drawer being pulled open next to her. Looking in the mirror, she watched his fingers glistening with her slick juices pluck a small wrapped packet from the drawer and carry it to his mouth to rip it open. Her lips curved slightly, enjoying the knowledge that he was as eager as she was.

"Stay!" Rafael tersely commanded as he lifted his restraining hand to help roll the condom over his thick shaft.

Seconds later, Mia felt the broad head of his penis press inside her narrow opening. Her head rolled back in delight as his invasion filled every nook and cranny of her body. Those blue eyes widened from the burn as his body neared hers, stretching her wider than she'd ever felt before.

"Rafael," she breathed, frozen in place on the counter. "Oh!" she gasped as he thrust forward sharply, meshing their bodies fully. She panted in reaction to the feeling of being completely possessed by the handsome man who leaned over her.

He paused for a few seconds, seeming to enjoy the squeeze of her muscles around him. Rafael's dark eyes met hers in the mirror. "Hold on, my sweet."

It was the only warning she received. While her mind processed his words, Rafael showed Mia exactly what being his possession meant. His hips pulled back before plunging fully into her. Pausing at each inward stroke to grind his pelvis against her swollen clitoris, Rafael pushed her pleasure higher as he sated their bodies' demands.

Mia reached forward to brace her hands against the counter as she met his thrusts eagerly. Her eyes devoured his body and expressions as he stroked and caressed her back and bottom.

She tried to emblazon this memory in her brain so she'd never forget. The pleasure that he inflicted on her body soon pushed any other thoughts from her mind. She could only feel and respond.

When Rafael finally relaxed his ironclad control to join Mia's last climax, the young brunette wilted over the vanity, her body overcome with the orgasms that Rafael had evoked from her. Eyes closed, Mia felt him slump over her body, supporting her with one muscular arm wrapped around her waist.

They rested together for several long minutes. Mia could feel his thudding heartbeat against her back. As much as Rafael wanted Mia to believe that he was aloof and distant, he had enjoyed her. She smiled softly against the towel and breathed deeply—sandalwood.

Her new favorite scent.

<hr>

SLIDING FROM HER QUIVERING CHANNEL, Rafael paused for several seconds, feeling bereft of the captivating squeeze of her body. Mia had fit him like a glove. Her response had been perfect, fueling his desire. Together, they had found unequalled pleasure.

As he'd plunged into her tight channel, Rafael had traced the redness of her bottom. She looked beautiful wearing the marks of her submission. He would need to discipline her regularly. Mia needed to feel his touch—both soft and harsh.

Now squeezing the punished flesh, he enjoyed hearing the soft gasp of pain from his exhausted possession. *She is mine!* Reveling in that thought, Rafael leaned over to press a kiss to one red buttock, allowing his tongue to swirl lightly over a small patch of blistered flesh.

When she pressed back against him even in her exhaustion, Rafael rewarded her. Lifting her body into his arms as Rafael turned her away from the reflection, he carried her into the bedroom. He enjoyed the feel of her curled against his chest as her arms linked around his neck to hold on. Once at the foot of the mattress on the floor, he released the arm under her knees to allow her toes to reach the carpet.

"Stretch out, my sweet. It is time for you to sleep," he instructed. Rafael waited as she struggled to follow his directions.

"Can't I sleep with you?" she finally asked.

"No, my sweet. On your mat." His tone was definite and commanding. The pleasure he had found through taking her body would not sway Rafael from what he knew she needed.

This time, she didn't hesitate but lowered herself to the mattress. Closing her eyes immediately, Mia crashed into sleep. The slow, even expansion of her rib cage gave away her slumber to the man who monitored her closely. He knew her mind took refuge from all that had occurred since her arrival.

Smiling at the realization that her ability to rest signaled that she trusted him completely, Rafael paused in place to enjoy the delightful scene before him. Mia was exactly who he had been seeking. Her body was as pleasing as her mind and submission.

He strode to the armoire and opened the large doors. Withdrawing the soft blanket that his housekeeper had laundered for him, Rafael spread the soft material over the sleeping figure. The corners of his mouth tilted up in as she mumbled his name, rubbing the fabric against her cheek as she dreamed. He enjoyed knowing that his presence had invaded her thoughts even when she slept.

Forcing himself away from Mia, Rafael returned to the bathroom to step back in the shower to rinse off their combined juices. When he returned to his enormous bed, he switched off the lights, plunging the large room into total darkness. Sliding in between the crisp sheets, he listened to her soft breathing before rolling to his side and deliberately clearing his mind to drift into sleep.

21

W aking on her mat at the side of Rafael's enormous bed, the silence clued Mia in that she was alone in the room. To double-check, she scurried to her knees to peek over the edge of the thick mattress. Seeing no one, Mia dropped back on the padding and turned over to curl into a ball on her side under the soft blanket. She barely remembered him covering her with it when he'd tucked Mia in bed.

Mia smiled as she squeezed her slender thighs together. She was definitely sore from his lovemaking. He had been right. Sex between the two of them had not been mundane. It had been more than she'd ever imagined. Rough and urgent, he had skillfully used her body but still ensured that she experienced as much pleasure as her body could endure.

She'd never had a lover like Rafael. Even thinking about it now made her shiver in delight. *I will not lose him*, she vowed fiercely.

Finally yielding to the pressure of her full bladder, Mia forced herself to walk into the bathroom to use the toilet. A few minutes later, she stood at the mirror, bemused by the image she projected in the glass. Her eyes held a glimmer of sexual satisfaction, making her look soft and happy. The young woman turned slightly, looking in the mirror to see the bruise marks from his gripping hands on each side of her hips. She smiled at the signs of his passion on her skin as her fingers lightly traced the dark splotches.

Ruefully, Mia thought of all her makeup back in her apartment. She wanted to look her best for Rafael. Mia settled with cleaning her face and washing away the traces of their lovemaking from between her thighs. After untangling her hair, she set the brush back on the counter. Walking back into the master bedroom, she found something waiting for her. Mia rushed to the bed to snatch up a gorgeous blue sundress lying across the tangled bedclothes.

She twirled to hold it to herself in front of the long mirror attached to one wall. The dress was incredible. The exact color of her eyes, it made her already big blue eyes look larger. She quickly unzipped the back and pulled it over her head. She struggled to close the zipper and only managed it up to her shoulder blades. Already it was easy to see that it fit perfectly, as if he'd had it tailored just for her.

Almost skipping in delight, Mia hurried down the hallway toward Rafael's office. The silky material brushed lightly over her bare nipples and bottom. Her lack of underwear seemed scandalous under the beautiful dress, and Mia laughed at herself. She'd been nude for days, and now wearing this dress, she felt more naked.

When she reached the office, Mia found the door closed. Hesitating, she debated between waiting, knocking, or slipping inside. His deep voice calling through the wooden door solved the problem for her.

"Come in, Mia," he ordered.

Happily, she turned the immense doorknobs and pushed the doors open. Meeting the eyes of four men seated inside, Mia felt her excited smile freeze slightly on her lips. "Oh, I'm sorry. I didn't know that you were busy" She excused herself, starting to back out the doors.

"Come here, my sweet," Rafael directed.

Hearing the steel in his voice, her feet obeyed. Mia walked slowly toward her lover, smiling slightly as that word bounced into her head. When she reached the side of Rafael's chair behind the enormous desk, he stood and held a hand out for her with a proud smile.

"Gentlemen, this is my Mia. She is just in training now, but I am very pleased with her." The men nodded pleasantly at Mia. "Turn around, my sweet. Let me finish zipping your dress. It looks very nice on you."

With the back of the dress closed, Mia looked at Rafael for direction. What was she supposed to do now? When one of the handsome men's eyebrows raised slightly, she knew this was a test. Crossing her fingers that she was doing the right thing, Mia walked behind his chair and sank down to sit on the mat next to his desk.

She held her breath as Rafael reseated himself. When his hand smoothed over the back of her hair briefly before turning back to restart the business conversation she had interrupted, she knew she had chosen the right option. Mia sat quietly listening to the words flying around over her head but couldn't follow the professional exchange.

Her eyes landed on the bottom drawer of his desk. The one that he had pointed out to her as having materials for her. Quietly, she pulled the drawer open. The quality furniture opened without a whisper of sound. Her face colored, remembering the loud slamming sound she'd forced from this drawer and the punishment and pleasure that had followed.

Peering inside for the first time, Mia found a breakfast cereal bar lying on top of a sketch pad as well as a pencil set. Quietly pulling all three from the drawer, she closed it silently. Turning around to sit at the edge of her mat and leaning back against the large desk, she scooted as close to his chair as she dared.

Opening the sketchbook and pencils first, Mia loved the smell of the heavy paper and the graphite and wood pencils. She had drawn nothing for years. Art had been her first love. Her father had left money in his will for her to go to college, but only if she chose something more stable like business over art. Now holding the first pencil in her hand, Mia realized how much she missed it.

She peeked up at Rafael's profile. How had he known? It was almost scary how much he knew, but Mia wasn't afraid. Inside, the lengths he had gone to know everything about her thrilled her. With a smile, she studied the lines of his face before setting the sharpened pencil point to the paper.

Mia drew until her hands cramped around the pencil. Knowing that she had reached her limit for the day, she quietly replaced all the supplies back into their packages before stowing them neatly back in her drawer. Suddenly exhausted, she lay down on her mat and listened to the conversations going on above her.

The first group of men were soon replaced by another. A teleconference followed that intense business-planning session. Rafael's focus and hard work amazed Mia. Whether he was working on his computer or talking to people around the world, Rafael never took a break.

Several hours after her arrival, she retrieved her sketchbook to write him an urgent note. Keeping it under the surface of his desk, Mia lifted the note and rested her hand on his knee. At his faint nod, she scurried to the restroom in the master suite and returned to find a cold bottle of water and a bowl of grapes on her mat. Rafael did not stop for lunch. Mia stroked his calf lightly as a silent thanks as she settled back down to eat and drink. To her delight, his fingers had stroked back over her hair, acknowledging and appreciating her presence.

When the ancient grandfather clock in the hall tolled seven times, Rafael closed his computer for the evening. Pushing back his chair, he stood and held out a hand to help her from the floor.

"It's time for dinner, my sweet. Are you hungry?" When she nodded eagerly, he instructed, "Go wash your hands and face. There is a restroom through that door that you may use when you are in my office," pointing at the large wooden door to the right of his desk.

"Do you remember how to get to the dining room?" Rafael asked with a raised eyebrow.

"Yes. I know where it is," Mia responded with a smile. She'd always had a wonderful sense of direction. Take her anywhere, and she could retrace her steps again. This skill had come in handy often.

When she came back into the office, it was empty. Mia stepped into the hallway and walked toward the dining room. When she passed the large entryway, she hesitated. This was her chance; she could escape. Taking three steps toward the frosted glass panels at each side of the large wooden doors, Mia hesitated before forcing herself forward.

She should want to leave. He had kidnapped her and brought her here against her will. Mia remembered pressing the yes button on the glowing computer screen. Her eyes filled with tears, recognizing that touching that screen had been the most daring thing she had ever done —something wickedly honest and just for herself.

Reaching out to trace the embellished metal door levers, Mia shook her head. She had always done what others said she should. Her life had been guided by what was expected and proper. What others thought she should do.

Here with Rafael, he was in total control of her life. But he offered her a life filled with pain and pleasure—thrilling her more than anything she had ever experienced.

Her hands dropped from the metal, and she turned around, putting her back toward freedom. She chose Rafael. Her eyes lifted from the tiled floor to meet that man's dark gaze. The corners of her mouth curled slightly at the praise she could read on his face.

Her ability to read his expressions made the feeling of passion and desire in the pit of her stomach relight. He'd allowed her to know him. Mia knew that was rare for the very reserved man.

More importantly, he'd allowed her to make her own decision. Who knew how long he had watched as she had debated whether to make a run for it? Mia walked forward, feeling the cold granite under her feet and the swish of the silky fabric against her bare skin.

"Hi, Rafael. Sorry to take so long. I bet you're starving," she said to break the silence.

The captivating man just held out a hand to her. "Come, my sweet. It's time for dinner."

When she placed her hand in his, Rafael pulled her close and wrapped one arm around her slim waist. She inhaled deeply, enjoying that scent of sandalwood and underlying male that always surrounded this bewitching man. He escorted her to the dining room and delivered her to the chair next to his. As she sat in her appointed place, Mia's eyes closed in delight at the light touch of his lips against her hair. *A kiss!*

Rafael had learned many years ago to push extraneous thoughts from his mind to focus on the business at hand. He had allowed himself to be aware of her movements, however. She had learned so much since her first appearance in his office. While he had enjoyed training her, Rafael realized he was proud of how far she had progressed.

He had deliberately tested her. Standing in the shadows, he had observed as Mia had recognized that she could free herself. His breath had frozen in his chest watching her fingers touch the handles that could release to allow her to escape. As she turned, he exhaled in relief, surprising himself.

Rafael knew she was important to him. He had spent a lot of time and energy in planning and carrying out the beginning of her training. His reaction to her decision to stay with him proved that he not only wished her to stay for more than just the superficial time expenditure. Mia had made her mark on him in a very short time.

Escorting her to dinner, Rafael found himself asking for her opinion of the business meetings to which she had been privy. While she had not totally focused on the conversations, Mia had mentioned small things which he had found insightful. The pitch of a businessman wishing Rafael to join a new venture had included the repetition of several key phrases. Mia had noticed and even begun tallying them as she drew.

"I'm not sure exactly without looking at the sketchbook, but I believe it was over twenty times. My thought was that he seemed to be almost trying to say it enough for you to believe it just from his words alone."

Making a mental note to scrutinize the proposal thoroughly, Rafael stroked the soft skin of the young woman's hand and wrist. He had not expected gaining beneficial insight from Mia. This was an oversight on his part. The investigations he had completed before bringing the young woman to his home had revealed her intelligence. Time spent with her was enlightening.

Catching his heart beginning to soften, Rafael created space between them after dinner. "My sweet. I have some additional work to finish this evening. I will walk you to my room where you will shower, brush your teeth, and immediately lie down on your mat to sleep."

"It's early, Rafael. Can I stay with you in your office? I'll be quiet," she promised.

"No, Mia. It is your bedtime. I will be there in a couple of hours. Come." He captured her hand and walked briskly through the hallways. Once through the doors, he dallied long enough to turn on the warm water in the shower and help her undress. Steeling himself from her allure, he sent Mia into the spray before tearing himself from the delightful view through the clear glass.

His office had never felt so empty before. Throwing himself into his work, Rafael attempted to distract his mind from the young woman who slept above him. For once, his ironclad control failed him as his thoughts lingered elsewhere.

22

————

Mia was pleased with her portrait of Rafael. She had labored to capture the essence of the magnetic man for three days now. Finally, she had captured that glint of passion in his dark eyes and the faint line of approval that she always hoped to see on his firm lips. Glancing up at the focused businessman, she wondered whether she should show him. Would he find her skill pleasing?

Nervous at revealing her artistic skills after such a long lapse in drawing, Mia closed the sketch pad with a firm snap. The sound drew Rafael's attention. His hands pushed against the edge of the desk to roll his chair away from his computer. He finally took a break. To the young woman's even greater surprise, those strong arms reached down to pluck her from the mat at his feet.

"I will stop working early today. There is a special event happening tonight, and we both need time to prepare ourselves," he announced with a smile.

"Really? Here?" she asked in absolute shock.

"Yes, my sweet." A knock sounded on the thick office door. "Good timing. They are here for you. I want you to allow them to take care of you. I selected all of their preparations carefully," he warned before calling out, "Come in!"

The man who Mia had deemed the butler entered. His reserved formality was wrapped around him, as always. "Sir, the team you selected is here. Would you like them to escort Miss Mia to one of the guest quarters to prepare?"

"Thank you, Anthony." Rafael lifted Mia to her feet before standing as well. "Follow Anthony, and I will see you tonight," he promised, giving her a slight spank on the bottom.

Mia took several steps toward the door before looking back at the standing businessman in his well-tailored suit. At his meaningful nod, she joined the people standing in the hall.

"Hi, I'm Mia," she introduced herself as she tugged the fuchsia minidress that Rafael had left for her to wear today down her thighs just a bit more. She had not been self-conscious of all the flesh that the dress revealed before now.

"Hi, Mia. I'm Sebastien, and this is Angel and Shadow. We're going to make you sparkle. Come on. We've got a lot to do." Linking his arm with hers, Sebastien whisked her along, chattering constantly. He finally took a break from his remarks about politics and the weather when they reached the guest room.

As the butler opened the door, Mia jumped in to ask, "What are you doing to me?"

"Oh, darling. You have a treat in store for you," Sebastien said, tugging her through the doorway before turning to speak to the lanky man in the group, "Shadow, will you and Angel bring all the supplies in, please. Start with mine. A new haircut is definitely in order."

As his two obvious assistants headed back to the entrance, Sebastien pulled Mia over to sit at the end of the bed. "Okay, darling. Your very generous man has ordered a complete makeover for you." He paused to lift a hand to her chin, turning her head at different angles.

"You have very good bones to work with. That will make our job much easier. So, here's the rundown. First, I'll cut your hair. Then, it's off to the bathtub for you to soak and soften all these rough edges," he shared, cupping her elbow and running an appraising thumb over the calloused skin. "A pedicure, a manicure, waxing, makeup, and you will sparkle in your new gown."

"My new gown?" she asked. Her head was swimming with all these plans. What in the world was going to happen tonight?

"Oh, you'll see that later." Sebastien smiled knowingly. "That man of yours has exquisite taste. It's the exact gown I would have chosen for you."

Noise in the hallway caused the enthusiastic man to bounce to his feet. Angel and Shadow entered pushing a dolly stacked with plastic storage boxes.

"Perfect!" He lifted the heavy blue one off the top and started to carry it into the bathroom. Stopping in the doorway, he turned to look at Mia in surprise as she stood in place. "Well, come on. Step one, haircut."

23

————

Three hours later, Mia posed in front of the large mirror. Fascinated by her appearance, she could not believe she had become the woman who looked back at her. Sebastien had cut and styled her hair in an elaborate updo that looked sophisticated and sleek. The makeup that Shadow had applied had widened her already big, blue eyes while making her lips look as if she would invite a kiss at a moment's notice. The gorgeous sparkly gown nipped in at the waist and clung to her hips, giving her an hourglass figure. They had erased any hint of mousiness that had lurked.

Only Mia knew about the intimate treatments the team had given her. Her body had been waxed of all body hair, buffed free of any rough skin, and massaged with a thick cream that felt so good and made her skin glow with health. She had clung to the thought that Rafael had ordered all these treatments when Sebastien's orders had exposed her nude body to the entire team throughout the afternoon. She wanted to please him.

The team's professional demeanor had reassured her that this was all normal procedure for them. Their actions proved that they were not bothered or particularly interested in her body. Sebastien had held her hand through the painful and intimate waxing. Now at the end of all their preparations, Mia had begun to consider all three as friends. Their chatter as they gathered all the supplies from the bathroom and bedroom indicated that they would see her often.

Mia glanced down at her nails. Gone was the frivolous pink polish with white flowers. Shadow had painted them a deep navy to match one of the shimmering colors in her gown and added one shimmering, white crystal that caught the light as she moved her fingers. Mia didn't know why they reminded her of her first days with Rafael, but that glisten mirrored the spotlight in the darkness that heralded his attention. Her toes in the sky-high heels mirrored the design.

Waving goodbye at Sebastien, Angel, and Shadow as they departed, wishing her luck in slaying the crowd, Mia pressed a hand to her thudding heart. She looked around the beautiful room that had been filled with activity for the last three hours. Now in the quiet, she had time to worry.

Smoothing a hand over the sparkling gown, she felt the soft dress liner touching her bare skin. Sebastien had refused to allow her to ruin the sleek lines of the long dress by wearing anything under it. Mia felt very exposed by the tight fit of the beautiful dress.

A faint scent made her twirl around to look at the doorway. That hand at her heart pressed a bit tighter to her chest. *Goodness, he looks delicious*, Mia's brain trumpeted inside her head.

Dressed in a coal-black tuxedo, Rafael stood in the doorway, appraising her with a pleased smile. He held one hand out to her and waited silently for her to walk self-consciously toward him. As she stood in front of him, Mia waited for him to say something, but he just looked at her.

Finally, her nerves forced her to speak. "Rafael. Say something, please. What's going on?" she asked in a trembling voice.

The debonair man simply tucked her hand into the crook of his elbow and led her out of the bedroom and down the hall. With each step, Mia could hear talking, laughter, and music growing louder. At the entrance to a large room, Rafael stopped to allow Mia to look at the swirl of activity.

There had to be thirty people filling the large drawing room.

Gowns flounced and twinkled as good-looking men paid special attention to the beautiful women. The variations in dress captured her attention before something else drew her contemplation. A small quartet played softly in the corner as everyone enjoyed chatting with each other. Mia looked at Rafael, trying to figure out what was happening.

"My sweet, I would like to introduce you to our friends," he said as a loud voice cut through the noise.

"Ladies and gentlemen, Rafael Montalvo and his Mia have arrived."

Mia looked over to see Anthony acting as the announcer. He gave her an encouraging nod as Rafael swept her forward into the gathering. Collecting a glass from the waiter, Rafael pressed the flute of champagne into her hand as everyone eagerly approached to chat with their host and meet his companion.

Clinging to Rafael's side, Mia soon abandoned any hope of remembering people's names. Everyone was charming and complimented Rafael on her beauty and poise. Little did they know that she was panicking inside at the press of people around her. Mia struggled to know what was acceptable and where she would make an error.

"Rafael, may Elizabeth give Mia something? My Little girl loves presents and wished to share with her new friend." The dashing, silver-haired gentleman held his companion's hand.

Mia's eyes flew from the middle-aged woman dressed in a short gown with thigh-high socks. Her graying hair was beautifully arranged in ringlets around her face. *She looks—charming and very sweet!* Smiling at Elizabeth, Mia wished to know more about her.

"Of course, Vincent," Rafael allowed, drawing her attention back to the conversation.

Elizabeth stepped forward and held one hand out with a small object on her palm. "I hope you like it."

Carefully, Mia picked up the black stone. It was warm from the woman's hold and seemed to radiate heat into her fingers. "It's so hot," she exclaimed as she turned it over in her hand.

"Everyone always thinks the darkness is cold and lifeless." Elizabeth grinned as Mia's jaw dropped in shock. "That proves them wrong." The older woman waved as she was pulled away to allow others to greet the hosts. The childlike gesture further enchanted Mia.

When Rafael held out his hand, Mia promptly turned over the smooth rock. She watched him tuck it safely into his pocket before turning to greet the next couple. Mia hoped she would get it back.

Finally, it appeared that they had almost met everyone. One last couple approached; they were almost a perfect reversal of Rafael and Mia. The Nordic man led his companion forward. She was a full-figured blonde whose thick hair was braided to fall over one shoulder, extending to her waist.

Smiling pleasantly at Mia, the gentleman's eyes did not linger on her trim figure showcased in the sparkling dress. His arm wrapped around the blonde's waist, snuggling her curves to his hard angles. As in all the couples whom she had met, Mia sensed a deep commitment between the two.

"Eric, I am so glad that you could join us," Rafael said smoothly, stepping forward to pat the man on his shoulder. "Alaina, I'm glad to see you feeling so well." He nodded at her.

"Thank you for inviting us, my old friend. I see that you found her," Eric said with an assessing glance over Mia's form. "She is lovely."

"She is more than lovely, Eric. She is my one. I remember when you captured Alaina, Eric," Rafael replied with a smile.

In shock, Mia looked at the dark man at her side. *Eric had captured Alaina? Had all these women been taken as she had?* Mia wondered, allowing the words to sound only inside her mind as she looked around at each couple.

A thousand questions burst into her mind. Mia stepped closer to Alaina and whispered, "He abducted you?"

"Shh!" Alaina warned, looking nervously at Eric.

"I can't ask you any questions?" Mia persisted.

"Mia, Alaina has chosen to be with me for a very long time. Our twelfth anniversary is approaching quickly." Eric smoothed the back of his fingers over Alaina's cheek in a soft caress.

Mia noticed the beautiful woman focused only on him as Eric began speaking once again, "Over the years, she has learned how to avoid displeasing me."

"She is exquisitely trained, Eric," Rafael complimented.

Trained? Mia's mind whirled with discordant thoughts. One part of her envied the obvious commitment this man had made to his wife. The blatant deviation from the accepted way everyone was supposed to be—independent and rely on themselves—clashed in her mind.

Rafael ran warm fingers down her chilled flesh, reminding her of his presence. Her independent life had been lonely. With him, she'd allowed herself to be free of societal norms of behavior. In such a short time, Rafael's approval and attention had become the most important part of her life. *Is this the same for Alaina?*

Eric's words pulled her focus back to the present. "You are new to this lifestyle. I don't believe I am overstepping when I suggest that you watch and learn from others. Take note of their warnings," Eric lectured.

"My Mia is very intelligent. She has already learned to heed the important lessons I share with her," Rafael praised before adding, "However, there are many things remaining for her to learn."

A silver bell rang, piercing the friendly conversations. "Come, everyone! It is time for dinner," Rafael explained. He tucked Mia's hand in the crook of his arm once again and led the couples into the large dining room. On this evening, the large table held many more than the two place settings of their typical solitary meals. The handsome host walked to the head of the table and seated Mia as usual on his right.

In the bustle as everyone found their seats, Rafael leaned close to Mia to whisper, "You must remain silent during dinner."

Mia looked at him in shock. His confirming nod told her he was very serious. The young woman jumped slightly as one of the waitstaff reached around her to unfold her napkin and place it on her lap.

Automatically, she opened her mouth to thank him but caught a warning look from Rafael. Her mouth closed with a snap.

The men began to talk. Mia listened with half her attention as she looked from woman to woman, noting the change in their demeanor from social butterfly in the predinner gathering to become silent and almost invisible at the table. Each woman's eyes focused on her plate rather than looking around as Mia was doing. Mia heard a couple of silvery tickles of noise and looked around curiously as she tried to figure out the source. No one else seemed to react to the sound.

Not understanding the women's reserve, she picked Alaina to stare at. Mia willed the friendly blonde to look up at her. Minutes passed. As they served the soup around the table, Mia finally saw Alaina shifting uncomfortably in her chair. Finally, the curvy blonde looked up to meet her eyes. Immediately Mia could read the warning in those wide eyes that looked back at her, and Alaina barely shook her head no.

Rafael leaned over to take away her soup spoon and drop it on the floor in a familiar ringing sound that brought a few men's attention to the host. Mia's face flushed bright pink under their reproachful glance. "Eric," he said conversationally.

Mia watched in horror as Eric picked up Alaina's soup spoon as well. The second silver spoon tinkled quietly as it struck the floor. The blonde's eyes rolled up to the crystal chandelier over the table before lowering back to the white tablecloth.

As everyone dipped their spoons into the delicious soup, Mia watched Alaina flip her thick braid over her shoulder before leaning in to lap delicately at her soup. Aghast, Mia turned to look at Rafael. Finding him watching her with a solemn expression, Mia opened her mouth to speak.

Without waiting for the sound to emerge from her lips, Rafael leaned over to pick up her salad fork and drop it to the floor as well. One raised eyebrow met her look of disbelief as her eyes rose from the silver fork on the ground. "Eat your soup, my sweet. Soon, everyone will watch and wait for you to finish so staff can serve the next course."

Trying to determine her choices, Mia heard several spoons scrape indelicately across the bottom of the bowl. Everyone would finish soon. Glancing back at Alaina, she discovered that the blonde had finished her soup and Eric was carefully wiping her face.

Looking around the table, not a single woman looked up. None of the men protested in the least. The professional conversations between them continued. No one was going to help her. Mia slowly leaned over to extend her tongue into the bowl. The delicious flavor of the soup burst over her tongue as she tried to eat the food delicately without a spoon. Lifting her head slightly, she eyed her knife, thinking she could scoop up the thick mixture on the wide blade.

Rafael's voice interrupted her thoughts as she sat up in her chair. "If you lose a third piece of silverware, I will remove your beautiful dress, and you will eat the remainder of your meal in the nude." He nodded to a trembling brunette at the far end of the table.

Her companion continued to speak with the other men around him as he unzipped the back of her dress and slid the garment off her shoulders, letting it fall to the ground. Her escort then captured both her wrists behind her back, thwarting her attempts to hide her body by slumping forward. He whispered something into her ear. Immediately, the brunette on display nodded somberly. She stepped out of the dress and waited until the man had reseated himself. Then, gracefully, she sunk to her knees and moved under the table.

As the conversation continued to flow companionably around the table amongst the men, Mia looked down the front of her beautiful dress to the bowl of soup in front of her. She had not seen the other woman's infractions that had resulted in her loss of clothing and relegation under the table. Mia knew that Rafael always meant what he said.

Slowly, she leaned back over her bowl to lap at the delicious soup. It was impossible to keep her face from being smeared with the thick mixture. She didn't dare sit up until she had finished the entire bowl. Sitting back, she wildly grabbed for her napkin to wipe her chin dry. To her surprise, Rafael was there immediately to clean her face with his napkin. She smiled tremulously at him, appreciating his care. Her heart skipped a beat as he nodded approvingly at her.

The clatter of dishes drew her attention away from his face. Glancing around the table, she discovered that everyone had finished and had waited just as Rafael had informed her. When she sat back against her chair, the servers removed all the bowls and placed the salad course in front of them.

24

H is Mia had many lessons to learn. Rafael watched her lap at the delicious soup. She was quick and understood quickly that she wanted to follow his directions. The consequences grew in severity with every poor choice. This first foray into their society would be the hardest for her.

When she lifted her beautiful face, he had immediately cleaned the remnants of the dish away. Her eyes reflected her appreciation of his care. It had been a learning process for all those present tonight. Rafael had chosen the attendees carefully to include those in varying lengths of time together. Mia had many examples to follow and those to avoid.

The men were important figures from the world of business and commerce. Movers and shakers in the world's economy, they were all linked by the bond of their particular attractions. Some he had known for years, and others were newer acquaintances. Each year, their number grew as new men were carefully vetted before their invitations to join arrived.

The Kings of Darkness had existed for hundreds of years. Dating back to the times of the Vikings who had pursued their mates ruthlessly, the KOD now included men from all continents. Beside their predilection for complete dominance, one characteristic bonded all those invited to join the group. Only the most powerful would ever be considered for admittance.

Beyond secretive, the group had maintained a secret identity from everyone. Quite a feat in today's electronic world, this elusive presence underlined the amount of power reflected in its ranks. No one would risk exposure of themselves or others. Their lifestyle was integral to each man's existence.

Tearing his thoughts away, Rafael focused on his beautiful companion as the next course arrived. Picking up his salad fork, he watched the realization dawn on Mia's face as she noted the empty spot in front of her. When her eyes flashed to his after dashing to the utensils still lying on the floor between their chairs, Rafael nodded once in confirmation.

Deliberately turning to ask Eric a question, he allowed Mia to make her own decision. When her head dipped toward her plate to grasp a lettuce leaf between her white teeth, he rejoiced internally. Her submission emblazoned itself on his mind. Relaxing his guard, he listened to the conversation flowing across the table.

"Conrad, I'm sorry. I only caught the name of that company as you spoke. I was recently approached by Travis Consulting. What can you tell me about them?" he asked, leaning slightly forward with interest.

"Beware, my friend. Travis Consulting is a new player that is making the rounds in the real estate world. While all appears aboveboard, there is nothing but rot under the polished presence," Conrad Elbert shared.

The petite redhead at his right sat perfectly trained with her eyes on her plate. Conrad was one of their senior members. his hair was now perfectly silver while a few strands of matching hue had been allowed to infiltrate Stephanie's vivid natural color.

Changing the conversation after everyone made mental notes of the company whose chances of doing business with any other KOD had just evaporated, Conrad shared, "I am glad to see you've found your one, Rafael. How is her training progressing?"

From the corner of his eye, Rafael observed Mia freeze in place. She visibly kept her head turned down to her plate as she struggled not to look at the man who inquired about her. "Mia has learned so much. She pleases me more each day," Rafael praised before adding more that would test Mia. "Her skin marks beautifully."

"You have chosen wisely, then. My congratulations. My Stephanie has enriched my life. Our second grandson was just born two weeks ago." Conrad nodded to a smiling man across the table. "Michael's son. He's a bit over the moon in love with the chubby little guy and ready to discipline his Catherine again, I'm sure."

"Stand, Catherine," the handsome younger version of Conrad commanded. Everyone clapped when he unzipped her cocktail dress to reveal crisscrossing red marks across her back. When she had resettled in her chair, he shared, "Her punishments relieve the stress of motherhood for Catherine. She is much happier now."

Rafael could feel the vibrations wafting from Mia as she struggled not to look up. He made no moves to prevent her from acting on her impulses. To his delight, her muscles relaxed, and she plucked a carrot from her dish. Her desire to eat normally overrode her curiosity. He ran an appreciative toe up the back of her shapely calf to reward her and watched the corner of her lips curl into a smile.

Vowing to host more gatherings for the group, Rafael glanced around the table. A movement captured his attention. Elizabeth stood with tears coursing down her face. Vincent emptied a linen napkin on the table. Green beans rained down from the cloth.

As the conversations around the table continued, Rafael watched both his Mia and now sobbing Elizabeth. The latter stepped out of her gown. Leaving it puddled on the ground, she walked to the closest corner of the room and pressed her nose against the cool paint. Elizabeth displayed her already reddened bottom to the room as the waitstaff distributed chocolate mousse for dessert.

Rafael subtly gestured to Anthony when Vincent signaled to him. The butler glided away and returned in a few minutes with a glistening piece of peeled gingerroot. When it was placed before Vincent, he nodded his thanks before carrying it over to further attend to Elizabeth.

Mia kept her eyes on her chocolate mousse.

25

Later as Rafael bid goodbye to all the guests, Mia stood quietly by his side. She'd figured out quickly that the social time before the meal had been the only part of the gathering where the women could talk freely. Three women walked into the cool evening warmed only by their male companion's arm around their waist, their garments draped over his other arm. Mia glanced down at the beautiful dress she wore, thankful that she had quickly heeded the rules as Rafael explained them to her.

"Come, my sweet," the impeccably well-dressed man encouraged as he steered her up the stairs to his master suite.

Quietly, Mia nodded. Grateful for his supportive arm, she was exhausted. She teetered on the unfamiliar high heels as she climbed the staircase that seemed twice as high as it had earlier in the evening.

Rafael quickly removed their clothing, leaving them in a messy pile on the floor. When Mia protested the care of her beautiful dress, Rafael just smiled fondly and ushered her into the shower stall. His knowing hands caressed her slick, wet body as he removed all the traces of makeup and washed her body. Mia twisted in delight as his hands explored the bare skin and treasures now on display thanks to the waxing she had endured earlier.

"Rafael?" Mia protested as his hands roughly turned her to face the beautiful tiled wall. The tantalizing man didn't answer as he held her in place with one forceful hand as he reached above her head to a small shelf. Mia heard a packet being opened and smiled against the tiles, welcoming his intimate touch.

Lifting her to her toes, Rafael thrust fully into her body. This time the sex was rough and brutal. The care that Rafael had shown in the past to push her arousal into pleasure was absent. Mia lifted one hand from the wall, intending to touch herself so they could climax together.

"No!" His rough voice in her ear made her flatten her palm against the wall again. "You lost your chance to orgasm the minute your spoon dropped to the floor. Learn to follow my directions completely, and pleasure is yours." He finished quickly, shouting his climax from behind her.

Mia leaned against the cold tile, aching for completion. Aroused and unfulfilled, tears streamed from her face. When he whispered that he had planned for her to share his bed that evening and his disappointment in her, Mia vowed to act according to his wishes fully in the future.

Aching and alone, she lay on her mat next to his bed, listening to his steady breathing. Mia shivered, uncovered. Rafael had even taken her blanket away. Tears rolled from the corners of her eyes as she berated herself. Finally vowing to do better, Mia fell into an uneasy sleep.

Sometime during the enveloping darkness of the night, the prick of a thin needle roused her slightly before she succumbed to the chemicals.

26

A nightmare of loss and unhappiness woke Mia with a jerk. She catapulted up to sit as she looked wildly around her incomprehensively. "What?" she whispered into the dawning light that filled her apartment's bedroom.

She was at home. Mia's mind rejected that thought automatically. This wasn't her home. Her place was with Rafael. "Why did he bring me back here?" she whispered as confusion filled her brain. Did he not want her anymore?

The thought of her computer burst into her mind. Tossing back the covers, she ran on feet aching from the high heels she had worn just a few hours ago to her laptop and impatiently waited for it to power on. As soon as it connected to the internet, she sent Rafael a message.

"Please, Rafael. Come get me or tell me where you are! I want to be with you. I'm sorry I didn't follow your directions. Please! Don't leave me here."

She stared at the bright screen in front of her, mentally urging him to respond. Twenty minutes later, no response had appeared on her computer. As she checked the time once again in the corner of her laptop, Mia groaned as she noted the date. Her vacation was over. Her boss expected her back at work today.

Mia needed to get ready to go. During the time with Rafael, she'd only thought of her job and friends at the beginning. The last several days, she realized with a jolt that she hadn't thought of her old lonely life at all. Rafael had ruled her thoughts and attention.

As the minutes passed and she risked being late, Mia dragged herself to her closet to choose clothes to throw on. A sparkle of blue and silver caught her eye. With a cry of despair, Mia pushed aside the hangars to reveal her beautiful dress. Pinned to the shiny garment was a thick piece of drawing paper. Her heart sank at the sight of the handsome face she had grown to love. Tears poured from her eyes. Rafael had kept nothing to remember her by.

She forced herself to dress in a businesslike pantsuit and pulled on flats. Grabbing her dead phone and a charger, Mia ran from her apartment to drive like a crazy woman to the office. Between speeding and wiping tears from her face, she barely avoided two accidents.

As she raced by, the young woman missed the concerned looks of the other workers in the cube farm that made up her division in the company. Swiping the note from the back of her chair, Mia sat down to power on her computer. She sighed in relief as she logged in one minute ahead of her scheduled time. A familiar face peered over the partition beside her.

"Hey, a tough vacation, was it? I don't think I've ever seen you without makeup. Not that you need it, of course."

The male voice of the man she'd flirted with for several months sounded whiny and young. She looked at him with red, tear-filled eyes, uncomprehending his friendly banter.

"Wow! That was a tough vacation. Something's wrong with your eyes. You must have an infection or something." There was an abrupt break before her colleague continued. "Did you even brush your hair? I've got a comb if you want to borrow it."

Mia's hand smoothed automatically over her hair. She reached for her purse and discovered that she had left her apartment with only her keys, phone, and charger. Suddenly worried, she wondered if she had even locked her door. Mia dropped her head into her hands and wished with everything inside her to be back with Rafael.

When she opened her eyes, she saw a small crowd of other employees standing around her cube looking concerned. Mia tried to pull it together. "Hi, everyone. The electricity was out in my building. I woke up so late. In my rush, I forgot all those things you have to do to come to work. Sorry, you'll have to put up with me in my natural state," she said, trying to joke.

"Come on, Mia. I've got some emergency supplies in my purse. Let's go to the bathroom and get you put together a bit better," a friendly voice offered as she wrapped an arm around Mia's slender waist and urged her into the restroom.

Mia survived the longest day of her life. Finally, back at home, she rushed to check for a message from Rafael. As she sat down at her computer, a blinking line appeared on the screen.

Soon, it will be time to decide. Will you choose Dark or Light?

Frantically, she raced to email back. "I choose you. Please, Rafael. Come get me."

Soon appeared on her screen.

A light flashed on in the hallway, catching her attention. She ignored it, willing Rafael to answer her. Nothing. No message popped onto her screen. The bulb extinguished and then lit again.

Mia stood slowly from her chair and walked into the short hallway. From there she could see all her small apartment. One by one, she watched the light fixtures illuminate and darken. Mia smiled. He was here.

Rafael hadn't forgotten her. She wrapped her arms around her slender body and hugged herself. Mia rushed to find the portrait she had drawn and carefully detached it from the dress.

27

R afael leaned back in his office chair. He had refused to erase the bits of her that remained. The mat beside his bed, her drawing implements in the bottom desk drawer, they all awaited Mia's return. Her absence had carved a hole in his heart. There would be only one cure.

He knew that Mia would need to make her own decision. The next time she came to join him would be forever. It was a weighty choice. She would have to give up all that her previous life had entailed: job, friends, apartment. Could she decide to center her life around their relationship?

Movement in her apartment drew his attention away from his thoughts. Feeling the corners of his lips rise, Rafael watched Mia slide into her lonely bed. Next to her sat an object she had carried around the apartment with her since her return. She picked up the framed sheet of drawing paper sitting on her nightstand.

Holding it to her heart, Mia closed her eyes and whispered, "Rafael, I will do anything to pass this test and be back with you. Please, I need you. I'm so lonely without you."

As he watched her press her lips to the image she had created, Rafael lifted his hand to touch his mouth with two fingertips. She would earn her kiss. Confidence flooded his mind. Mia would be his forever.

The room darkened, and Rafael turned off the massive display on the wall. It was time to prepare. Mia would be home with him soon. He would not rush her last chance to escape his control if that was what she wished. But shortly, she would be his completely.

Taking the small black stone from his desk drawer, Rafael placed it about his keyboard. Pulling up his calendar, he began to make arrangements. When it was time, he would be ready.

28

One month later, Mia pushed back her chair from her home computer. Her eyes studied the framed portrait next to the laptop. She hadn't heard from Rafael Montalvo since that last word. *Soon.* Mia's life had slowly returned to her old normal. Boring and routine, she longed for the discipline of the fascinating man who had brought life to her secret fantasies.

The young woman had exhausted every means of searching for the man she craved so badly. The only bit of interesting information she had discovered was that he owned the building where she lived. She wondered if he lived or worked there during the week. *Maybe up on the penthouse level?* She searched everyone's face each time she entered the elevator.

Mia knew somehow that living here explained how she'd come to his attention and how he now monitored her activities. She began talking to him as if he were in her apartment with her. *It might be crazy,* she'd thought, but it made her feel close to him once again.

"Rafael, could today be the day that you come get me?" she asked, just as she did every day. Mia held her breath, waiting for some response. Rafael had always signaled her in the darkness by adding light to show her he was there. Her eyes darted all over the apartment, willing something to tell her he heard her. The one-sided conversations that she had initiated in the past had not resulted in any response.

Click! Click! Click! Tonight, one by one, every light source began to glow.

Bursting from her chair, Mia jumped up and down in excitement. Quickly, she moved to the center hallway so she could see throughout the apartment and celebrated each new spotlight that made her space blaze with light.

Rafael! she shouted in excitement.

Racing to her computer, Mia threw herself into the chair and watched the screen. She never turned off the laptop these days in fear of missing his message. Seconds passed, turning into minutes.

"Please, Rafael. I need you. I belong to you. Won't you come to care for me?" she asked the blank message screen.

Inhaling in disbelief, she smelled sandalwood. Her hands pressed against her heart as she slowly turned around to face the man who stood behind her. When he held out his arms to her, Mia lunged from her chair to wrap her arms around his neck. Unintelligible joyful noises echoed in her throat as she clung to his body. Her lips pressed urgent kisses against his chest.

"My sweet. I want you to be sure. If I take you away this time, you will be with me forever," he warned, easing her away from his body to meet her tear-filled blue eyes.

Her head nodded slowly, without a second's hesitation. "I want to be with you. I want to belong to you, Rafael. Please."

"As you wish, my sweet. I will be glad to have you with me for I have missed you as well," he answered, sending shivers of happiness through her mind and body. "Last chance, my sweet," he offered as one hand reached into his tailored jacket pocket unbeknownst to her.

"I wish to be with you," Mia answered, stepping closer to him. At the prick in her neck, her fingers tightened on his shoulders. Almost immediately, she began to crumple to the ground. Once again, he did not allow her to touch the floor as he caught her with one arm.

Mia missed seeing the large arched mirror in her living room swing open as he triggered the hidden lever. The young woman whom he had chosen on sight when she appeared to tour the small apartment had always been within his reach. Despite what the manager had said, this apartment had stood empty for years as Rafael waited for just the right resident to apply.

She would need nothing from her previous life. Rafael paused only to pick up a gilded picture frame from her desk. He left everything else.

29

H er fingers traced the patterned weave on the mattress beneath her. Mia lifted her head from the padding to sniff fabric covering her shoulder. Sandalwood. She smiled into the absolute darkness. He had brought her back with him.

Fighting off the wooziness from the drug that had knocked her out once again, Mia forced herself up to sit against the wall. Her fingers fumbled with the buttons on her blouse as she took off her clothes and folded them neatly on the concrete at the foot of her mattress. Soon, she sat naked on the mat as he preferred.

Mia didn't try to track the time. She dozed in her position, allowing the drug to work its way through her system. When she finally roused clearheaded, she inhaled the smell of him. "Rafael," she whispered softly.

White light cascaded from the fixture above her padded sanctuary, piercing the blackness. Mia pushed herself to stand by the edge of the mat as she peered into the darkness that surrounded her. "Rafael, thank you," she whispered as the shape of broad shoulders solidified before her eyes as he approached.

"You belong to me," he sternly reminded her, walking steadily forward.

"Yes!" she agreed, holding her breath as she hoped for her dreams over the last month to come true.

"Yes," he confirmed before gathering her into his arms. His lips captured hers. His dominant kisses made her cling to him. They revealed the depth of his emotion and ignited the passion that flared between them. Only now would he share his kisses with her.

His hands roamed over her body. Cupping her buttocks, he lifted her from the cold floor and lowered her to lie on the mattress below them. Slowly, he removed his tailored jacket. After pausing for a few seconds to stare down at her nude body lying at his feet, Rafael reached into the inner pocket and withdrew several small packets. He dropped them to her mat.

Mia stared at the number of condoms as he stood waiting. His possession would be unrestricted. Shivering with delight as she met his observing gaze, Mia watched as Rafael dropped his jacket on the floor. He unfastened his cuffs and continued to rid himself of the elegant trappings of a successful businessman. Soon, he stood nude before her adoring blue eyes.

As he lowered himself gracefully to kneel on the padding next to her, Rafael clasped her reaching hands and held them securely over her head to scan the slight body before him once again. "I will take much better care of you than you chose to in the last month," he declared as his dark eyes noted the hollows in her body that had not been there before.

"I'm sorry," she whispered, afraid that he was not pleased with her body.

"There will be a punishment for not caring for what is mine. First, however, I need to feel you against my skin."

Dropping to one elbow, he pressed her hands to the padding as a warning to keep them there before running a caressing hand down her body. His fingers discovered just how delighted she was to be with him. Rafael's lips captured hers as the spotlight snapped off to leave them wrapped in darkness.

Mia smiled against his lips as the words etched into the wooden door above them flashed into her mind:

May you escape
to the freedom that
darkness offers.

30

W hen Rafael awoke the next morning with the much-too-thin Mia in his arms, he kissed her sweet lips to wake her. He had used her body repeatedly through the night, leaving his mark on her body. No part of her had been off-limits as he claimed her as his.

He stood and triggered the spotlight at the side of the room. The padded bench sat centered in the light. Mia pushed herself up to sit and looked at him in distress as he dressed. Her brow wrinkled as she watched him roll his shirtsleeves up over his muscular forearms. Without questioning, she took the hand he extended to her.

Rafael pulled her easily to her feet and lifted her body into his arms. "You are too thin, Mia. You did not take care of yourself."

"I tried, Rafael. I was too upset to eat as I waited for you. What if you'd never come?" she explained with tears welling in her eyes.

"I will take care of you now, my sweet," he reassured her, carrying his precious burden to the bench. "Into position," he commanded after setting her feet on the concrete.

"But... I was so good. I waited faithfully for you," she pleaded.

Rafael knew she watched as he chose a flogger with long, thin strips of leather. Turning, he smiled inwardly as she shivered before him. "Five additional blows for failing to follow directions. I believe you have forgotten your training, my sweet."

Holding her eyes, he waited. It was easy to see her thoughts flashing through her brain. Mia's expressive face gave away her emotions, ranging from fear, anger, and finally, submission. To his delight, she finally nodded before dragging her feet to the apparatus and arranging herself into position.

Deliberately moving at a slow pace, Rafael tethered her in place, pulling the restraints snug. He brushed a tender hand down the length of her spine. Bruised fingerprints scattered along her body. His possession had been rough and thorough last night.

Gliding his fingers over the slight curve of her buttocks, Rafael explored the private space between her spread thighs. She jerked slightly at his touch, revealing that she was sore after being repeatedly taken. Her body welled with fresh slick juices immediately, revealing her true reaction to being bound. He pressed two wet fingers to her small entrance between her buttocks and pushed against the tight ring of muscle until she groaned as he breached the entrance.

He stood next to her body for long seconds as she struggled to relax around his invasion. The lapse in her training created a barrier that only she could break through to submit totally. He waited, giving her time. Slowly, her body ceased pushing against him and relaxed around his fingers. Allowing an additional minute to pass, Rafael tested Mia. To his satisfaction, she softened over the supportive bench.

"Very good, my sweet," he praised, sliding his fingers from her bottom. After cleaning his hands, Rafael stroked the limp leather strips across her bottom and up her torso. Then raising the flogger, he brought it sharply down over her shoulders.

"I'm sorry," Mia apologized as her body tensed at the blow.

Again and again, Rafael lowered the flogger with quick, rapid flicks of his wrist. The skin of her back blossomed with red lines standing out against the pale flesh. His eyes never left her as he observed her reactions. When she melted over the bench, exhaling hard, Rafael knew he had erased her transgressions. Each blow had been for her. She'd needed his punishment and reassurance.

Tears fell freely from her wet lashes. Her back and buttocks burned from the impact of a thousand thin but wicked strands. Ever errant thoughts that had haunted her during her time away from him had been erased. She'd tried to do as she'd thought Rafael would like. Sometimes, she'd been weak without him. The punishment had cleared her of any misdeed during their separation.

Mia felt Rafael unfasten the bonds holding her to the padded frame. Wrapping his powerful arms around her, he lifted her slight form back into his arms. This time when his lips pressed softly against hers, Mia felt as if she'd earned the intimacy. She lay still on the familiar mat as he massaged cream into her abused skin, those hands stroking her body until her eyelids drooped with weariness. He had not allowed her much sleep last night.

"Are you ready for the light, my sweet? Or do you need more darkness?" he asked softly.

"Darkness," she admitted honestly in a whisper-soft breath.

"Sleep, now. Let the darkness wrap around you and comfort you."

Nodding, Mia heard the subtle sound of his footsteps as he left her. She closed her eyes in exhaustion. Her body hummed from his mastery. There was no inch of her flesh that remained unmarked by him. Reassured by his dominance, Mia allowed herself to sleep deeply.

Rafael filled her dreams. His scent followed and tantalized her. Pain and pleasure combined to soothe her soul. The darkness surrounding her did not judge. It provided solace from the judgment of others. Nothing mattered but the wants and desires of Rafael and herself.

Waking to find a beam of light dissecting the darkness to stop inches from her mat, Mia pushed herself up to sit as she preferred with her back against the wall. She watched the light. Somehow this bit of light made everything else look darker. As something new, Mia heeded its importance. Rafael was sending her a message.

"What, Rafael? What do you wish me to do?" she called into the obscurity. The wisp of light glided over the floor. Maneuvering herself to her feet with a groan, Mia followed it. Her memory told her she was headed to a different section of the lower level that she had not seen.

Walking past the bench and table, the light led her through a hidden doorway into a small chamber. Once inside, warm water began to fall from above to wash over her body. Mia turned in a circle, dousing herself in the cleansing flow. She watched the beam slide across the wall to point out a small indention with a bar of crude soap. Picking it up, she rubbed it over her skin and dropped it to the floor as her skin burned.

"Rafael, it hurts," she shouted into the darkness as she desperately worked to rinse the strong cleanser from her skin. When the discomfort eased, Mia turned in a circle, trying to find the sliver of light again. Total darkness greeted her at each side.

"What am I doing wrong?" she asked, mentally reviewing her actions. The light had shone until she touched the soap to her skin. No, that wasn't correct. The white sliver vanished when she dropped the harsh bar.

Squatting down to the shower floor, she slid her fingers over the wet tiles. Finally, her fingertips brushed the bar. Instantly, the sliver of white reignited.

"You want me to use this soap?" she questioned, holding the bar far from her skin. When there was no reaction, Mia knew she was correct. Gritting her teeth, she spread the penetrating lather over her body, urgently rinsing it from her skin as quickly as possible. Deliberately, she avoided her privates and her face.

No light shone. Gritting her teeth, Mia lathered her face and rinsed it desperately. With tears streaming down her face, she squinted into the darkness. Waiting. When still the beam did not return, she slid the bar through her pink folds and between her buttocks. Bouncing from the stinging pain, Mia splashed and splashed again frantically until the horrible feeling subsided. Her head drooping in reaction to the ordeal, she glanced down at her feet.

Light!

Whirling in the shower stall, she found Rafael standing behind her. She walked forward into the soft towel he held extended for her. His hands gently dried her abused skin before dropping the damp material. Her view narrowed to the hollow of his throat as he scooped her into his strong arms. Mia nestled her face into the curve of his neck and breathed in deeply. His sandalwood scent soothed her mind as he carried her from the darkness. Freed from any impurity from her contact with the outside world, Mia knew she was where she belonged.

"Thank you," she whispered as they emerged into the light. His response made her heart thump erratically. The feel of his lips against her damp hair unburdened her soul. It did not matter that he had returned her to the apartment to ensure her ability to choose. He wouldn't send her away again.

31

S he woke in the late afternoon. Pushing against the familiar mattress lying next to his bed, Mia sat up. She stroked her skin, appreciating the silkiness of the nourishing cream that Rafael had slathered onto her skin before directing her to lie down. The soft blanket draped over her lap, attesting to his care.

Rising to her feet, she ran her fingertips over the soft cotton tunic stretched over the bed. Almost skipping with delight, she hurried to the restroom to use the toilet, wash her face, and brush her hair. When she found a tube of tinted lip balm on the counter, she spread it over her lips with a deep groan of delight. Rafael thought of everything.

Soon, she descended the stairs to his office. Finding the door open, she scooted inside and circled around the back of his desk. Never making eye contact with the visitors, Mia sunk down into her usual spot and rested her head on Rafael's thigh.

As he led what sounded like an intensive conversation, Rafael threaded his fingers through her hair and caressed Mia's scalp. When he tugged at a handful of the brunette tresses, she groaned softly and froze, not wishing to interrupt the important conference. She relaxed slightly when he continued to speak without hesitation.

Against her forehead, she felt Rafael's cock begin to stir. Unable to resist, she angled her face to watch the process in fascination. Generously endowed even at rest, Rafael's body beguiled her. Mia loved his toned and muscular body completely, but she definitely had one favorite part. She licked her lips as she watched the broad head push against the fine wool of his trousers.

Rafael wrapped a hand around her cheek, and she turned her face to press an ardent kiss against his palm. Shifting slightly, he traced her lips with the tip of his thumb. Mia opened her mouth to nip his manicured fingertip. When he invaded the warmth of her mouth, she pulled his digit deeper into her mouth. With swirls of her tongue, Mia welcomed his incursion, enjoying the taste of his skin.

When he rolled his chair back slightly, Mia sat back, afraid to be in his way. Glancing up at Rafael's face, his composed expression startled her. There was no visible sign of his rising passion on his face. The strategic conversation continued over her head. She had the impression that he was not pleased with the visitors and had called them in as a warning. They, however, had not picked up on the subtle language Rafael employed.

As she eased away, Rafael signaled her to stay in place with a shake of his hand. She watched as he stroked his engorged shaft and shifted himself slightly away from his zipper. To her amazement, Rafael flicked open the button at his waist and grasped the tab at the top of the metal teeth. Lowering it slowly, he freed his heavy cock to burst from the confinement of his slacks.

Frozen in place, Mia didn't know what to do. Surely he didn't want her to pleasure him here... during a business meeting? He answered that question by wrapping his hand around the back of her head and urging her forward. When she pulled away, his fingers tangled in her hair and pulled strongly in silent warning.

Nodding even though she knew he wasn't watching, Mia moved closer. She lapped tentatively at the broad tip after wrapping her hand around his shaft. Rafael's flavor burst over her tongue. The taste of his skin was magnified here from the heat of his body.

Her fingers looked miniscule, not spanning the girth fully. His body throbbed within her clasp as if welcoming her touch. Mia could feel herself becoming wet in response to his arousal. He had never allowed her to touch him freely. Fierce pride burst through Mia. She had earned this. He was allowing her this intimacy.

She wanted nothing more than to bring him pleasure. The men on the other side of the desk did not matter. Only this was important. Mia wanted to gratify this man who loomed so large in her life. It was vital that he found her useful and beneficial.

Trailing the tip of her tongue from the tip down to the base, Mia nibbled lightly at the root of his cock. When his fingers tightened on her head, she knew that he enjoyed her attentions. She moved quietly to position herself between his spread thighs. Her body nestled in the cubby underneath his desk. Reaching inside his slacks, she cradled his balls in her hand and freed them from confinement. Mia tugged the heavy globes slightly away from his body as she leaned in to taste him once again.

This time, she swept her tongue around each orb before sucking one at a time into her mouth. The creak of the chair in front of the desk startled her, and she automatically lifted her head away from his body. Rafael tightened those punishing fingers tangled in her hair, giving her a painful warning to continue before releasing her.

Sinking back towards his body, Mia understood that she was to ignore all that was going on around her. She allowed herself to be drawn magnetically back to the broad head of his cock. After swirling her tongue to taste the droplet of arousal that had gathered there, Mia stretched her lips around the tip to engulf it. As she lowered her head over his thick erection, she felt Rafael's body move as he shook hands with the two men who reached over the desk. There was no way that they could miss seeing her service Rafael.

Funny, the thought floated through her mind. She did not care in the least. The only person's opinion that mattered was Rafael's. Even hearing them commented on how lucky their host was didn't bother her in the least. His guiding hand returned to the back of her head as Rafael excused himself from standing and asked the two men to see themselves out. Perhaps they believed they would have blackmail to leverage against the businessman in the future dealings. Mia pushed the idea from her mind. If Rafael had allowed them to see this act, there was a purpose in mind.

Wrapping her fingers around the opened waistband of his pants, Mia tugged, silently asking him to remove the barrier. Rafael stood as the door closed, pressing himself deeper into her throat. She quickly yanked his slacks to midthigh as she sat back on her heels. She clung to his body, gripping his upper thighs with her hands for stability as he drove into her mouth.

"Touch yourself!" he demanded. When she didn't shift a hand between her needy thighs, Rafael pressed deeper into her throat, blocking her supply of oxygen. When she looked at him fearfully, he repeated his words. "Touch yourself. Bring yourself to the edge of an orgasm. Do. Not. Come." That final sentence emerged in a staccato of stipulation.

She snatched one hand from his thigh and lowered it to glide through the wetness between her legs. Her eyes drifted closed as he used her mouth. Again, those punishing fingers tugged at her tender scalp. Her eyes widened and focused on him.

He watched her. Observing every reaction, every expression that crossed her face, Rafael continued to thrust into the warm depth of her mouth and throat. She did not attempt to mask her emotions. Somehow, she knew he wanted to see her struggle to take him and the growing arousal that built inside.

She could feel the tingles hovering just outside her reach. Mia quickened the movement of her fingers while increasing the suction on his shaft. She hoped that he would give her permission to join him in pleasure. She knew, however, that they needed to come together, or she needed to follow him. Punishment awaited if she came first.

"Now!" he roared as gushes of hot fluid jetted down her throat.

Swallowing desperately, Mia thrust two fingers into her pussy and felt her body leap into pleasure. Ecstasy burst throughout her body as her muscles clamped around her inserted digits. Mia suddenly understood. She wanted to serve him in whatever capacity he needed her. He made her feel more than ever before. She was his.

After several long moments, Rafael restored his pants and sank into his chair. Mia laid her cheek on his thigh and felt the corners of her lips curl upward as he once again cupped the back of her head, holding her close. She didn't move when he shifted forward to grab his cell phone as it rang.

ACCEPTING THE CALL, Rafael listened carefully to the cultured voice on the other end of the line. He brushed back the stray locks of brunette hair which had drifted across her face. Delicately tucking them behind her ear, he celebrated her return to him. He would not be an easy man to choose. He would demand all that she could give and more.

Decisions, he thought as he listened to the information. The two men who had just left hadn't even cleared his grounds before one had placed the call. Filled with the incorrect business data that Rafael had confidentially shared with them, they had contacted his competitor, a tycoon named Eric Atherton. Unaware that Rafael tested everyone, the two had sealed their fate.

A half mile from their office, a felon escaping from police custody darted into the road before them. Automatically, the driver swerved to avoid hitting him. Unfortunately, a large truck hauling rubble away from a nearby construction site had parked directly in their new trajectory. The resulting fireball had engulfed the interior immediately. There had been no survivors.

"Thank you, Eric, for taking care of this matter for me." His voice paused as the other man spoke. "Yes. I owe you one. Now, for more pleasant matters. Mark your calendar for the eleventh. I hoped you would be my best man as Mia and I marry. Mia will be delighted to have Alaina be her matron of honor."

Rafael met Mia's wide eyes when she sat up abruptly to look at him. "Yes, the wedding will be on the eleventh at five in the evening. Dinner to follow. The invitations went out this morning." After several minutes of idle conversation, he concluded the call.

"We're getting married?" Mia blurted.

"Yes, my sweet, on the eleventh," Rafael answered as he lifted her slight body and relocated her to the side in front of her drawer. As he turned on the large display before him to start the next call, he smoothed a hand over her head to soothe her. She'd totally forgotten about the men's unpleasant visit. Thank goodness her talented mouth had provided a pleasant distraction from the unpalatable conversation. "Draw me a picture of your dream wedding gown," he suggested as the screen illuminated.

"Mr. Midori, I am intrigued by your unique proposal," he greeted the business giant as the call connected. His full attention shifted immediately to the screen.

Mia followed his directions eagerly. Pulling out her sketch pad, she drew herself wearing the wedding gown of her dreams. It was simple and graceful, decorated with lace only at the edge of the sleeves and hem. The back dipped daringly to her low back.

An errant thought crossed her mind, and Mia grabbed the colored pencil to add a few small details. Red stripes across her back illustrated his possession of her body. Mia's fairy-tale wedding would differ from those in the storybooks. Who needed knights and dragons? She had Rafael.

32

The next morning when she awoke, Mia sat up to peek over the edge of Rafael's bed. Displayed on the elegant bedspread lay a pair of jeans, a pale yellow sweater, and pale pink intimates. She lurched to her feet in surprise. Rounding the bed, she ran a finger over the soft knitting.

Tearing herself away from the bed to run to the restroom, she thought furiously. *Why is he giving me regular clothes?* The deviation from her regular simple dress without undergarments concerned her. *Is he sending me away?*

Mia knew she would need to dress in the clothes Rafael had left for her. She shouldn't question his decisions, but... Was he tired of her already? What had she done wrong? She delayed in the bathroom as long as possible. Dragging her feet, Mia emerged.

"My sweet, I am ready to go. Why are you not dressed?" Rafael asked in concern.

"Are you sending me back to my apartment?" burst from her lips as tears began to course down her cheeks. She couldn't lose him. She couldn't.

"Come here, Mia," Rafael commanded, opening his arms to

capture her as she bolted forward to press her face against his suit jacket.

"I don't want to go, Rafael," she pleaded. Her heart pounded inside her chest. This couldn't be the end. She wouldn't let it. Steel stiffened her spine. Straightening in his arms, Mia lifted her face, still streaming with tears, to meet his gaze. "I won't go. I won't let you send me away."

She watched his concerned expression soften. The wrinkles of alarm faded between his eyebrows. His arms tightened around her as he leaned down to take her lips. The ardent kiss wiped away all questions in her mind as she responded to him passionately.

When Rafael lifted his head, triumph shone from his eyes. "You were going to fight for us," he marveled.

"Yes. You're too important."

"You are going nowhere, my sweet. I have claimed you for my own, and soon we will be wed. Have you forgotten the eleventh?" His hand stroked over her shiny hair and down her back to comfort her. "Your place is with me now."

"Then, why do I need these clothes?" she demanded, wanting to believe him.

"We have an appointment for blood tests and for you to be examined for birth control. I do not want any barriers between us from now on," he calmly explained.

"Birth control?" she echoed.

"There will be a time when I decide you should have a baby. Now is not that time. I wish to enjoy you myself for several years." His hand stroked between them to cup her stomach. "Then, I will enjoy planting my seed inside you and seeing my child grow within you."

After several quiet seconds, Rafael stepped away. "Dress quickly, my sweet. If we are late, you will see the doctor with fresh marks on your body."

Knowing how revealing the exam for birth control needed to be, Mia sprung into action. She stepped into the brief, lacy panties and pulled on the matching bra. It felt confining to wear the garments after dressing without them as Rafael normally directed. Zipping the jeans closed, she wiggled uncomfortably. With a sigh of delight, she pulled on the soft sweater.

"Go get your brush. You may fix your hair in the car. It will come in handy if we are late," he instructed.

Mia raced to the bathroom to collect the heavy hairbrush that he preferred she use. Weighing it in her hand as she returned to him quickly, she hoped that traffic would be light. She had felt the impact of the wide wooden back before.

RAFAEL CELEBRATED Mia's rebellion as he maneuvered the car through the heavy morning rush hour. The fire within her proved how perfect she was for him. Mia's submission was her gift to him. Just as he believed that she was the only woman for him, Rafael knew that Mia would never submit to another as she did for him.

Brushing her hair to a beautiful shine, Mia sat quietly next to him. When Rafael caught her checking the clock, he raised one eyebrow waiting for her question.

"What time is the appointment?" she asked.

"Yesterday, at ten o'clock."

"Yesterday..." She looked at him in horror. "We're already late."

"True." He watched her in between focusing on the traffic. She stared at the brush in her hand. Seconds ticked by as she made her decision. Slowly, she placed the brush in one of the drink holders between their seats.

The traffic thinned as they approached the large complex of office buildings. The doctor's office was at one corner. Rafael parked his car and picked up the hairbrush. Exiting, he rounded the car to open Mia's door and assist her out.

His arm encircled her waist as he ushered her inside. The hairbrush bounced against her clothing as they walked, reminding her of its presence and threat. At the desk, he identified himself and waited as the receptionist searched for his appointment.

"Ah, Mr. Montalvo. I see your appointment was yesterday, but you are on the priority list. I can take you back to a room immediately. We did receive Mia's previous health records. Thank you for sending them."

She stood and led the way to a room at the corner. "Mia will need to undress completely. The doctor will be in when he finishes with his current patient."

As the door closed behind her, Rafael held out his free hand. When Mia looked at him blankly, he directed, "Take off your clothes, my sweet." Reading her mind as she looked around the room, he added, "Dr. Waltham knows that you don't need a gown. We won't be here for long, and he will need to examine you fully."

When she stared at him in disbelief, Rafael set the brush down on the exam table and walked forward to lift the soft sweater over her head. Instantly, she stood placidly, allowing him to undress her. She followed all his directions instantly. Soon, her clothes were folded in a neat pile next to the brush.

"Very good, my sweet. Come, lean over the table so you can meet the doctor without a punishment looming over your head."

"What? You can't use that here." She pointed in horror to the brush.

Rafael raised one eyebrow and waited. When she didn't move immediately, he checked the time on his watch. A minute passed before Mia bowed to his wishes. Without a word, he helped her move into position with her breasts pressed against the cold vinyl of the exam table, her bottom aimed directly toward the door.

Tethering her to the table with a hand between her shoulder blades, he picked up the hairbrush. Rubbing it over her small bottom, he detailed her punishment. "We were ten minutes late today. I will take responsibility for the mix-up in days. You delayed a minute, so you have earned eleven swats. Cover your mouth, my sweet."

The first strike landed on her right buttock, and a gasp escaped from her throat before she clapped her hands over her lips to trap the sound. Two, three, four landed. Mia raised up on her toes as the pain began to build. Her hips shimmied back and forth, trying to evade the next swats of the hard, wooden hairbrush as Rafael counted to nine.

A click of the door and a rush of cooler air from the hallway drew Rafael's attention, "Dr. Waltham. One more and she will be ready for her exam," he greeted the white-coated man as Mia's struggles to free herself increased. Rafael easily held her in place.

"Hi, Rafael. I'm glad to see you and Mia," the friendly voice greeted them without acknowledgement or concern as he closed the door.

Mia cocked her head to listen but wasn't able to see the man behind her. The final punishing strike landed. She tried to stand as the hand on her back eased.

"Mia can stay in that position. I'll start with her bottom first," the doctor instructed. He moved to the side of the exam table and handed Mia a few tissues. "Here, my dear. I understand that sometimes discipline must be administered immediately. My Elizabeth is sometimes very naughty." He patted her shoulder before pulling on exam gloves with a snap.

"The rock," Mia sobbed, obviously putting the pieces together. She remembered him from the dinner party. She watched him squeeze a large dollop of lubricant onto his finger.

"Yes. You are correct. My Elizabeth brought you a present. You'll feel some pressure now," he warned in the same conversational tone. This time, Mia rose onto her tiptoes for an entirely different reason.

Twenty minutes later, the doctor peeled off the last of the gloves he would need for her exam. Armed with swabs from each of Mia's orifices and tubes of blood from the couple, the doctor wrapped up his very thorough exam. Rafael had enjoyed assisting the doctor through the various stages and had picked up several pointers for ensuring her care.

"You are a very lucky man, Rafael. Mia is healthy but underweight. I'm going to send home a sample diet for her. It's probably unnecessary with your incredible chef. He'll help her rebound to a more suitable weight," Dr. Waltham declared with a chuckle.

"Thank you, Vincent. We'll see you on the eleventh."

33

F rozen, the knob wouldn't turn. Mia wanted to bang her fists on the wooden barrier, but she knew it wouldn't help. Rafael had decided that she would sleep in the guest room where she had dressed for the party.

Turning to look at the luxurious bed, Mia simply wanted her mattress on the floor. She wanted to hear him breathe above her. Already she missed the smell of sandalwood that always enveloped Rafael.

Something black on the mattress caught her eye. Darting forward, she grabbed the small object from the bedspread and held it tightly in her hand. The black stone warmed quickly against her palm. "Thank you, Rafael," she called.

"You're welcome, my sweet," the soft answer drifted through the thick wood.

Gripping the stone, Mia clambered into bed and settled against the soft pillows. Immediately uncomfortable, she piled them carefully on the other side of the bed and pulled a blanket over her body. Sleep came quickly.

"HELLO, SLEEPING BEAUTY!" Sebastien's cheerful voice woke her. "Wow! Do we need to tame that bed head." He lifted the blanket from her body as Angel and Shadow brought in all their supplies. He scanned her naked body and sighed. "Okay, team. We have our work cut out for ourselves."

"Start warming the wax, Angel," he instructed, before turning back to Mia, "Go, girlfriend. Go pee. We all have to, first thing in the morning."

As Mia clambered from the bedding, he gasped dramatically at the sight of the fresh red marks crisscrossing her back. "That's going to take a lot of concealer."

"Nope, the marks stay according to the big boss," Shadow reassured Sebastien as he glanced over her back. "Go pee, Mia. I'll come in to start the bathtub soon. Those calluses are going to need some soaking time."

Mia fled into the bathroom to follow their instructions. The clinks and bashes of the plastic storage bins made her smile. She laughed at herself. The last time had seemed so unreal. Now, it was still out of her comfort level, but she knew and trusted them.

It appeared that Rafael had made up his mind and the wedding would happen. She shook her head, laughing again. He definitely moved quickly when he decided to pursue something. She could feel like a fox on hunt day, but she didn't. This felt right.

"Come on, snickers. Bring your laughter out here and share the joke," Sebastien called as he started turning on all the lights in the master bathroom.

Shadow had already set up the large padded table and was heating the wax. Even the threat of having the hair on her legs and nether area ripped out didn't faze her. Mia rushed forward to hug each of them before allowing Angel to help her into the warm water flowing into the tub.

"Okay, guys. You did okay last time. Can you help me knock Rafael's socks off this time?" she joked. Mia knew her limitations and just appreciated their help in looking her best.

"Challenge accepted."

Widening her blue eyes, Mia gasped at the united force of Sebastien, Angel, and Shadow ringing the large tub. They were serious. Grinning at their calculating expressions, Mia stretched out in the tub. The next hours might be excruciating, but the look on Rafael's face would be priceless.

Soon, the trio had everything arranged in the large room to their satisfaction. Angel sat down next to the tub to dip her project's hands into a paraffin bath. "What are you holding?" she demanded when Mia attempted to dip her fist into the wax.

Opening her hand to display the smooth black stone, Mia clamped it shut again when Angel moved to pluck it away. "I need to hold on to this. It's important."

When silence filled the room, Mia looked apprehensively from one face to another. Would they understand?

"I always add a small pocket in all the wedding gowns I create. Most brides use it for the old trite something old, something new, something borrowed, something blue. Perhaps in your case, this should be tucked safely there?" Sebastien suggested.

"Yes, please. I need to have it with me."

"Then, I will take this and safely stow it in its own special spot."

Slowly, Mia opened her hand once again to display the stone. With great solemnity, Sebastien removed it from her hand and left the room. Once she knew that he'd taken care of it, she relaxed back again in the tub. Immediately, Angel restarted her treatments.

"Thank you," she whispered when he returned.

"Everyone needs something. We understand that."

The room filled with the chatter of the three stylists. Mia put herself into their hands, allowing the trio to pamper and prepare her. Once out of the bath, they completed the intimate treatments. Then, Sebastien cut, washed, and dried her hair to a shine. So relaxed, Mia actually fell asleep as Angel painted her finger and toenails.

"Time to dress," Shadow announced as Sebastien styled her hair into an elaborate updo. He ushered her into the large guest room. When Mia's stomach growled, Angel produced a snack bar for her.

"We don't want you to faint at the altar," she declared, opening it for Mia.

"Can I see the dress?" the bride-to-be whispered.

"Soon. You need to put it on to see the special requirements that your groom ordered. Eat!" Sebastien urged. He knelt in front of Mia to smooth the silk stocking over each of her legs and up to ring her slim thighs.

When she had finished, Sebastien unzipped the top of the protective sleeve to pull out a sheet of sketch paper. "I believe this was your dream gown?"

Mia looked at her drawing, and tears welled in her eyes. Quickly, Angel leaned close to press tissues to the corners of Mia's eyes.

"Don't ruin your makeup," the cosmetician commanded, before whispering, "Your guy seems tough, but of all the grooms I've known, he seems to know you the best."

"He does." Mia nodded as she waved her hands before her face, trying to force the tears away. Finally, she had it under control. "Okay, I'm ready to see the gown."

Sebastien unzipped the garment bag to reveal a gorgeous wedding gown. The elegant simplicity took her breath away. He had brought her dress to life.

"It's beautiful, Sebastien. Thank you!" She stood, eager to put it on. As they lifted it over her head, Mia was enveloped in darkness. The lining of the white gown was pitch-black.

"Wait!" she begged, needing to absorb the symbolism of this gown. Rafael knew her better than anyone. Her heart ached from his caring touch.

Seconds passed as the stylists allowed her time to appreciate the dress fully. When Mia threaded her hands through the arms of the gown, they finished smoothing it into place. It fit her like a glove. As Mia looked into the large mirrors that had been moved into the room during the preparations, her breath caught in her throat.

Mia didn't recognize herself. Staring at the image in the mirror, she ignored the final makeup and hair touches. She stepped into her shoes and turned to look at the back of the dress. The vivid red slashes across her skin glowed in the frame of the dipping line of fabric. Rafael's absolute possession of Mia's body, heart, and mind would be on display as they stood at the altar.

"It's perfect, my dear," Sebastien sighed romantically.

"Are you staying for the wedding?" Mia asked, desperately hoping that the three would be there.

"It is our honor," the head stylist answered with a nod. His words echoed with the pleased expressions of Angel and Shadow.

A knock on the door drew their attention. "It's time," Angel announced, clapping her hands before making shooing motions at the two men. "Go sit down. Save me a seat on the aisle."

Angel escorted her to the large vestibule where Mia had stood so long ago with her hands on the carved metal doorknobs, sealing off the outside world. As the attentive woman straightened her dress and smoothed a lock of hair into place, Mia stared at the entrance to the drawing room where the ceremony would take place. Panic flashed through her.

"My stone. I can't do this without it!"

"Here." Angel brushed down the left side of her dress.

Something small pressed into Mia's body. Her hands immediately traced over the bump. Completely disguised, the stone was tucked close to her body. Mia fumbled into the opening that Angel revealed and withdrew the black stone. Closing her hand around it, she felt its warmth.

"Thank you," she whispered and tucked it back into place.

"Of course. Are you ready? I hear the music starting," Angel asked. When Mia nodded, she picked up the beautiful wedding bouquet and placed it in Mia's hands. "This smells so good. It reminds me of your groom," she added with a smile.

Lifting the bouquet to her nose, Mia inhaled. Under the heavy scent of the beautiful roses, she detected it as well—sandalwood. Rafael's scent lingered in her nostrils as she began to walk forward.

Rafael commanded her attention. His expression thrilled her. It was the same fierce possessive look Mia saw each time Rafael selected an implement from his arsenal. She was already his. As always, she walked forward into his care.

At the altar, Mia's heart leapt to hear Rafael say that he loved her for the first time. In her shock, she almost missed his special vow to care for her in darkness and in light. The light touch of his hand along the raised marks on her back ensured that she paid attention.

Without hesitation, she repeated the words back to him, giving her eternal pledge. She leaned against him for stability as he took her hand to slide on the gorgeous wedding ring. Formed of a single brilliant white solitaire surrounded by a scatter of black diamonds, it symbolized their relationship more than most.

His band? A wide black-and-gold ring that mirrored hers without the sparkle and shine. Mia slid it onto his ring finger, marking Rafael as hers.

EPILOGUE

"Thank you for joining me, brother." Rafael faced the gathering. His eyes never left his Mia. Her frequent glances his way completed the visual story. It was obvious to all in attendance that he was as in love with his new bride as she was with him.

"I couldn't miss your wedding day, Rafael." Miguel lifted his champagne flute to celebrate his twin.

"I have a present for you," the groom informed him before motioning to the hovering butler. Handing the leather pouch to Miguel when it was delivered, Rafael shared, "Father and Mother's apartments in the city now pass to you. Here are the keys and the details that our sire shared with me before his death. I hope that they will complete your life."

Miguel watched his brother's attention shift to Mia as she celebrated with two friends during the social hour. He had not become an active member in the Kings of Darkness. Glancing around the room, he nodded at familiar faces who he should have been surprised to see as participants but wasn't.

Taking another sip, Miguel gestured with the pouch. "Thank you, Rafael. I believe it is time to seek my one."

For more books and authors in the Leave Me Breathless Collection,
please visit WWW.LEAVEMEBREATHLESSBOOKS.COM.

Never miss a Leave Me Breathless release! Subscribe to our newsletter
HERE: https://leavemebreathlessbooks.com/subscribe

A NOTE FROM THE AUTHOR

Dear Reader,

If you've enjoyed this story, it will make my day if you could leave an honest review on Amazon. Reviews help other people find my books and help me continue creating more Little adventures. My thanks in advance.

I always love to hear from my readers what they enjoy and dislike when reading an alternate love story featuring age-play. You can contact me on my Pepper North FaceBook page, on my website at www.4peppernorth.club, or eMail at 4peppernorth@gmail.com.

I'm experimenting with Instagram, Twitter, Pinterest and MeWe. You can find me there as well!

Pepper North

ALSO BY PEPPER NORTH

Dr. Richards' Littles

A beloved age play series that features Littles who find their forever Daddies and Mommies. Dr. Richards guides and supports their efforts to keep their Littles happy and healthy.

Zoey: Dr. Richards' Littles® 1

Amy: Dr. Richards' Littles® 2

Carrie: Dr. Richards' Littles® 3

Jake: Dr. Richards' Littles® 4

Angelina: Dr. Richards' Littles® 5

Brad: Dr. Richards' Littles® 6

Charlotte: Dr. Richards' Littles® 7

Sofia and Isabella: Dr. Richards' Littles® 8

Cecily: Dr. Richards' Littles® 9

Tony: Dr. Richards' Littles® 10

Abigail: Dr. Richards' Littles® 11

Madi: Dr. Richards' Littles® 12

Penelope: Dr. Richards' Littles® 13

Christmas with the Littles & Wendy: Dr. Richards' Littles® 14

Olivia: Dr. Richards' Littles® 15

Matty & Emma: Dr. Richards' Littles® 16

Fiona: Dr. Richards' Littles® 17

Oliver: Dr. Richards' Littles® 18

Luna: Dr. Richards' Littles® 19

Lydia & Neil: Dr. Richards' Littles® 20

A Little Vacation South of the Border

SANCTUM

Pepper North introduces you to an age play community that is isolated from the surrounding world. Here Littles can be Little, and Daddies can care for their Littles and keep them protected from the outside world.

Looking After Lindy: A SANCTUM Novel

Protecting Priscilla: A SANCTUM Novel

One Sweet Treat: A SANCTUM Novel

Picking Poppy: A SANCTUM Novel

Rescuing Rita: A SANCTUM Novel

Needing Nicky: A SANCTUM Novel

Adoring Ali & Ace: A SANCTUM Novel

The Keepers

This series from Pepper North is a twist on contemporary age play romances. Here are the stories of humans cared for by specially selected Keepers of an alien race. These are science fiction novels that age play readers will love!

The Keepers: Payi

The Keepers: Pien

The Keepers: Naja

The Keepers Collection

The Magic of Twelve

The Magic of Twelve features the stories of twelve women transported on their 22nd birthday to a new life as the droblin (cherished Little one) of a Sorcerer of Bairn. These magic wielders have waited a long time to take complete care of their droblin's needs. They will protect their precious one to their last drop of magic from a growing menace. Each novel is a complete story.

The Magic of Twelve: Violet

The Magic of Twelve: Marigold

The Magic of Twelve: Hazel

The Magic of Twelve: Sienna

The Magic of Twelve: Pearl

The Magic of Twelve: Violet, Marigold, Hazel

The Magic of Twelve: Primrose

The Magic of Twelve: Sky

The Magic of Twelve: Amber

The Magic of Twelve: Indigo

The Magic of Twelve: Rose

Other Titles

The Digestive Health Center: Susan's Story

Electrostatic Bonds

Perfectly Suited

The Medic's Littles Girl

3rd Anniversary Collection

Tex's Little Girl

Marked Brides

Jax's Little Girl (Coming Soon!)

Santa's Naughty Helpers (Coming Soon!)

ABOUT THE AUTHOR

Pepper North is a hybrid author whose contemporary, paranormal, dark, and erotic romances have won the hearts of many loyal readers. After publishing her first book, Zoey: Dr. Richards' Littles 1 on Amazon in July 2017, she now has over fifty books and collections available on Amazon in four series.

Listed among Amazon's Most Popular Erotic Authors, Pepper has enjoyed trading off that coveted number one position with incredible authors. She credits her success to her amazing fans, the support of the writing community, and her dedication to writing.

Join the addiction…#peppered!

Printed in Great Britain
by Amazon

22042296R00089